WALKING ALONE

DILIP CHAKRABARTI

authorHOUSE®

AuthorHouse™
1663 Liberty Drive
Bloomington, IN 47403
www.authorhouse.com
Phone: 833-262-8899

Published by AuthorHouse 12/03/2020

ISBN: 978-1-6655-0792-9 (sc)
ISBN: 978-1-6655-0793-6 (hc)
ISBN: 978-1-6655-0796-7 (e)

Library of Congress Control Number: 2020922896

CONTENTS

ACKNOWLEDGEMENT

I have noticed that most of time nobody likes to discuss the influence or help what he received from others, it is a characteristic very prevalent among human beings. This type of denial I have seen a lot, where a person not only refuse to express the gratitude, often defames that benevolent person from whom he gained a lot. But for me it is very different, I learnt from my childhood the value of gratitude, strength of truth and I also learnt that admission of accepting help does not degrade anyone rather it shows the strength of character and respect for human qualities.

I should acknowledge the fact that if I was not hospitalized in Jalpaiguri, probably I would go back to Kolkata and never go to any pharmacy school and be a pharmacist. Deep down my heart I believe in destiny and my life in a way has been designed by the all mighty god.

My most sincere gratitude must go to Dr. P.K.Sanyal who opened the door for my professional education. Without his help and guidance my life would probably have taken a different path.

My friend Dr. Amal Banerjee's help was absolutely

indispensable when I established "Mrinmoyee Madhusudan Hall" in memory of my parents in Jadavpur University in Kolkata. My friend the then Town Supervisor Thom Kleiner took the initiative to help establish the "Chakrabarti Family Scholarship" in South Orange Town School District, Rockland County. Jay Garett, Trevor Ross and Harold Lester always helped me in my business venture with their expertise, I shall always remember their kindness and I express my heart felt gratitude for all of them.

My million thanks and gratitude must go to Mr. Sudhir Mukherjee who brought me to his place when I had no place to go from the NYC Airport and I shall always remain grateful to him for kindness to me.

My family life would never be so wonderful without the association of my classmates of Jadavpur University. Our families were known as "Pharmacy Group" among others in the area, this group is my pride and joy and I am grateful to be a part of this wonderful extended family away from my family of India.

Although being an ordinary human being, I had the privilege of meeting many great and famous persons like Swami Tathagata Nanda of Vedanta Society of New York City, Mural Bhai of Adya Peeth of Dakshineswar and many others whose friendship really enhanced my vision towards human life, this is my lifetime experience of learning process.

DEDICATION

My family has been the center of my life. My family includes my brothers and sisters as well. Among them, my parents, my wife, my daughter, her husband and their two children are the inner soul of my life.

To my mother Mrinmoyee and father Madhusudan: your love and affection have always nurtured me, your warm embraces gave me assurance and security. I always found peace and happiness in your bosoms. Love you both.

To my mother: your teachings: always respect a woman, her inner strength and foresight are the solid foundation of any family, I have always tried to follow your advice, my wife is the foundation of my family, her strength and wisdom are the strength of my family.

To my father: your teachings, devotion, honesty and sincerity are the strength of character, I always try to possess them. Your exemplary kindness is a shining star, I would like to follow but it is very hard to do so. I have always tried to follow your footsteps with your blessings.

To my wife: thank you very much for bringing the strength

and wisdom in our family, also thank you for traveling together in the journey of life and to do the same beyond.

To my daughter: you are our joy and pride, without you we would not be a family. Your husband and you have made our family stronger. Your son and daughter are apples of our eyes, we pray that eventually they be raised as decent and kind human beings. May Goddess Kali always shower her blessings on all of you. All of you have made our family bond stronger and eventually made our lives more enjoyable.

Finally, this book is dedicated to our grandchildren Lakshmi, Dominic, our daughter Pritha and our son-in-law Matt Rotundo.

FOREWORD

I was inspired to write this book by two very special persons of my life. Their experience, knowledge and depth observance of life are dramatically opposite. One of them is our daughter, Pritha who has entered the family life with her children, son Domenic and daughter Lakshmi along with her husband Matthew. The other person is Swami Tathagatnanda, a spiritual and holy man in his excellence of real knowledge of life and beyond.

One afternoon Swami Tathagatananda was supposed to deliver a speech in the NY Kali Mandir in Baldwin of Long Island, I went to bring Swamiji from Ram Krishna Mission of New York City. The drive was about fifty minutes long.

We were discussing about the decadence of Hindu Religion especially among Bengalee Hindu Families in USA and in West Bengal. Political situation influenced by communism was also one of the contributing factors for this decaying of religion. Although I was very concerned but Swamiji was not concerned at all. In his opinion Hinduism always passed through this type of era but in the long run Hinduism always survived with new vigor and influence.

Swamiji wanted to know when I came to this country, how were first few years of life in this country. I informed him first few years were very hard and uncertain, broken promises of friend almost put me in the street, however I was rescued by another good Samaritan who gave me shelter in his tiny place for the first night in this country, not only that he gave me food and assurance that he would help me in this dire situation. After listening to my suffering story, Swamiji advised me to write my story so that nobody else ever fall into this ditch and suffer like me. After listening to him, I told – Swamiji, I am not a writer, nor do I have the talent of literary excellence or guts to write, people would be laughing at my writing.

Swamiji differed with me and said – you would be writing for the new comers to this country, so that they do not fall into the helpless situation like you. Your book doesn't have to be a literary excellence, as long as it describes the events you been through and your readers can avoid such incident after perusal of your book. Even if one person can escape this type of situation, that is the success of your book, people will benefit from your book. They would appreciate your endeavor for writing the book. Do not hesitate, once you start, the rest will follow automatically, and the almighty will help you.

Swamiji was a very pious and spiritual holy man. When he asked me to write, to me it was a word from my God. I spoke to my wife about it, I gave a real good thought about it and I followed Swamiji's advice and one day after doing Pranaam to Swamiji I started to write the book and the rest is his blessings.

Some of the readers may identify themselves in similar

situations, but the characters and events are related to my personal experience only, although some imagination, some fiction and some daily life experience have been blended together, if any of these matches to someone else's, that would purely be a coincident and this matching is not intentional at all.

If the readers enjoy this book, it would be the greatest reward for my hard work which I have done to write this book. I shall accept any kind of opinion, good or bad with equal importance and pleasure.

PREFACE

In the wake of riots in East Bengal my father was compelled to leave his house and property in twenty four hours' notice from the Islamic Militants who threatened to kill every member of family, he took his family and left everything behind, consequently he became a pauper in next twenty four hours later. He moved to Kolkata, India with his wife and two children. No place to live, no money to use, his life was turned upside down, his family started to flow around like a straw in a speedy current of flooded river Family became extremely indigent and consequently life became very uncertain for this family.

As a young child the writer's schooling became uncertain due to financial crisis. Dilip engaged in selling onions, garlics, etc. in the local vegetables' market. This was not an ordinary act those days, it was rather very unusual. One day one of his customers wanted to know – why, instead of going to school, he was working in the market. Listening to him the customer asked him to see him in the local school after his work. This customer was none but the Head Master of the local high school and he took him in his school for studies. He also granted a free studentship for him. This is how his stopped schooling started to roll again. His daily routine, go to market, come back and go to school, come back and go to market again, come back and study and prepare for the school's home work at night for the next day. While in high school, he found a part time job as a clerk in the local government transportation system. Later on he joined the Pharmacy School in Jadavpur University and graduated from there. In middle seventies he migrated to USA and had to struggle hard in different hard adverse situations. In the early part of his life in USA he worked for NYS Government and later on started his business in retail pharmacy and in few years business started to sail well and since then he never had to look back, success according to his own definition, came to his door step. He became very happy and content with his life and family.

He wanted to share his good luck with them who did not have it. He started to share and support many philanthropic organization in West Bengal, India and in here also. Under his leadership NY Kali Mandir was established in Baldwin of Long Island. This is the first Bengali Temple established by Bengalees of New York who came from West Bengal, India. He always felt that it was his destiny and Ma Kali's blessings on him and his family, eventually his wife and he dedicated themselves completely to the service of the Goddess Ma Kali.

TROUBLE AT AMBER ALERT

———

D r. George Vargas moved to New York with his wife, Grace, many years ago from a small town of Africa. In the beginning it was very difficult for Vargas family to adapt to the new place, new society, and a new country. As time went by, this family started to put its feet on the ground of success. Family gathered money, fame and a little child named Vanessa. Years went by, Vanessa grew up to become a fine young educated woman. She did her Ph. D. in Microbiology and started to work for a Hospital in the same city where her parents were living.

Vargas family is very proud of their daughter Vanessa. Vanessa grew up with the human value system which was embedded in her by her parents. Vanessa is very popular among her friends for her pleasing personality and fellow feelings. She is very independent. Her parents live in the next town, about twelve miles from her home. Her parents requested her many times to babysit her daughter, Vanessa, when she goes to work. But Vanessa always politely refused their offer – Mom, I want to follow your footsteps, the way dad and you raised me without any family help, I want to fulfil my responsibility to raise Melissa by your son-in-law and me, I want to make you both proud of your daughter by being a responsible affectionate mother. Of course, if I ever need any help you two will be the first person to take care of Melissa. Finishing her sentence she embraced her mother and said – Mom, I love you very much, you are the best.

Listening to Vanessa her father George said – what about me, remember - I also love you.

Daddy, don't be so jealous, you very well know that I love you both very much. Mom gets little more because she feeds me with her good cooking. I hope you would not mind if I bribe her for good foods. This way you also can share those delicious dishes, so keep quiet, and let me take care of my mom. She hugged her mother very strongly. This is Vargas family at its peak of love, affection and caring.

That was supposed to be a bright summer morning but the sky was cloudy and gloomy. George and Grace were sitting in their kitchen. Suddenly it started to rain lightly but wind was blowing very strongly. George asked – Grace, I am going to make tea, would you like to have some?

Grace replied – yes, please. Then said – don't put any sugar for me, I will put it myself.

Why, you don't trust my trembling hands any more, yes, now a days they tremble due to my disease but they can still hold you tight, especially for you they can become strong again. Remember, when we were traveling in Arizona, you tripped and almost fell down and these hands firmly hold you steadily that day, and saved you from falling down, George stopped and smiled at her wife Grace.

Grace looked with all the affection in her eyes at her husband and said – George, the day you married me, I knew, I got my prince charming who will always care for me, who will always love me and carry me in his arms and make my life joyful forever and keep me in his heart forever.

Suddenly phone started to ring. George said – Grace, please answer the phone, I am making the tea. Grace picked up the phone and said – hello. It is their daughter Melissa. How are you all, Vanessa? – Grace wanted to know. Vanessa sounded little weak and worried. Grace asked – where is Pat? Pat is Vanessa's husband. What happened to you? You sound very weak.

Vanessa said – mom, he went to office. Mom, I am not feeling well and Melissa is little cranky and also has diarrhea. Every ten fifteen minutes, I am changing her diaper. I am giving her electrolyte. She should be okay. Mom, I have a presentation to make in my office and I must have to go to the office. Mom, how is daddy? Mom, I was thinking if you could babysit Melissa today. Can you come and pick her up now?

Hold on for a second, let me ask your dad – replied Grace. Grace explained to George that they have to pick up the most valuable person of their lives, their grandchild Melissa and they have to leave now because Vanessa has to go to her office. George asked – can I finish the tea? Grace said – no, when we come back with Melissa I shall make you a fresh cup of tea, now let us go. Then she talked to Vanessa – we should be in your place in next twenty minutes. We are on our way, see you soon.

Both reached Vanessa's home and noticed Vanessa is lying down in the couch and Melissa is playing nearby. Grace touched her forehead and said – what happened to you? Are you alright?

Ma, I do not know what happened to me but I feel very weak and I have to go to work because I have to make a presentation to a group who are from England, otherwise I would not go to office today – replied Vanessa.

Grace went to the kitchen and made a glass of Horlicks with milk and brought to her and said – drink this, you should feel better. Stop your dieting mania, eat healthy, you will never feel weak. I am your mother, please listen to me, I know what is better for you. She stopped and told George to get ready to leave with Melissa. George was playing with Melissa. Melissa loves to play with her grandpa. She did not want to stop playing. George told to Melissa – we shall play more when we go to our home. Bring your shoes, let me help you to put them on. Melissa said – grandpa, I can do it, I shall put them on by myself. She started to put the shoes on and after finishing she said – see grandpa, I know how to put on my shoes.

Melissa knows that she has to sit on the child seat. She sat there and started to buckle up with her little hands, but could not secure, she got frustrated and started to cry saying – grandma, sit belt. Grace said – Melissa, I am coming. She sat on the back seat of the car and secured the seatbelt and Melissa was happy, smiling and caressing grandma. George said – Grace, shall we start for the home? Melissa said – yes, grandpa and started to drink milk from the bottle, she behaves big. Grace said – George, your granddaughter gave you permission to go, they both smiled and George put her car on the go.

On the highway George saw a sign "AMBER ALERT". George said to Grace – Grace, there is an Amber Alert Sign. Someone has kidnapped a little girl and he is driving a white car. They did not give the make and number of the car. George noticed in the rear mirror view that a police car is coming very fast, he moved to the right lane to let the Police Car pass. Before Grace could reply to George, she noticed that Police Car is approaching fast to their car in the same lane. Grace worried and asked George – what happened, are you speeding? Why the police is behind us?

George said – I do not know why he is following me. Grace felt the anxiety in George's voice. Anxiety became real when the police asked George to stop. George moved to the emergency stopping shoulder and stopped his car. The Police Officer approached George's car and said – sir. May I see your license, insurance and registration?

George replied to the Officer – what is the problem Officer? I did not speed or anything? Then George handed over the papers to the Police Officer.

The Officer replied I shall let you know when I come back after checking of these papers. He took these papers and went to his car to verify the authenticity of them. George told his wife – I do not know why he stopped me. Little Melissa did not really understand what was going on and why grandpa has been stopped by police. She said – grandma, why grandpa stopped? When are going home? I want to go home. Grace gave her the bottle of milk and said – Melissa, please drink this milk and we will go home soon. She is four years old, she does not understand why her grandpa has to stop, she wants to go home soon and play with her dolls. In the meantime, the Police Officer came back and said – sir, please step out of the car. George came out of the car and said – Officer, what is the problem, why are you asking to come out of the car?

Police Officer replied – your car matches the description of the car of the Amber Alert that is why you have been stopped. In the middle of their conversation Melissa interfered and said to the police – let us go home, I want to play with my toys. Grandpa, please drive the car. Police replied to Melissa – yes honey, you will be with your mom and dad soon.

By this time George and Grace have realized that they have been stopped because police thinks that they have the kidnapped girl in their car. Now the grand parents have become the suspect of kidnapping in the eye of the police. Grace came out of the car and said – officer, we are the grand parents of this child. She is our granddaughter, our daughter and her husband are her parents. Our daughter is not feeling well, so we are taking her to our home. We shall babysit her today. George also pleaded – we are not kidnappers, we her grandparents, both of us are highly educated, I am a physician, I do not have to kidnap any child. Please let us go. Child is also not feeling good, she is upset, also wants to go home. Please ask the child if we are her grandpa and grandma. Please let us go and then you can start to look for the real culprits who have done this heinous crime.

Police Officer mockingly said – yes, right, a white baby is

your granddaughter, please don't give me that nonsense, I have called the detectives of crime unit, they will handle this case. He then called his office and said - two brown persons have a white child, they are claiming to be her grandparents, then looked at George and angrily said - please stop talking, and let me do my job. Grace told the Officer – why don't you ask the child if we are her grandparents. But he would not ask the child if they were her grandparents. He thought – he caught the culprits, solved a crime. Also said – I am not going to talk to the child. He is firm on his decision. Grace and George tried to explain to him that their daughter is married to a white guy and his name is Patrick whose family is from Ireland but the Officer would not pay any attention to these statements from them. He won't budge. In the meantime two other officers came took them under custody and fetched them to the precinct. After being treated badly by the police, George became very angry with this Officer, George demanded to see the In-Charge of this Precinct and said - can I speak to him, please?

Grace realized that this Officer will not listen to them. So, she called her daughter Vanessa and explained the situation they are in. In the meantime other units of police came and arrested George and Grace and charged them for committing a crime of kidnapping and took them to the police precinct. In the precinct police started the process of arraignment. This Police Officer put this couple in an embarrassing position, maligning their personal dignity because they are not white, because their grandchild is white, these officers are very stubborn and irrational and she has to do something to resolve this problem.

While they were being subjected to this process of humiliation, Vanessa came to the precinct and asked her husband Pat and father and mother-in-law to join Pat and Vanessa in the precinct. The whole family came to precinct and demanded to see the child and Vanessa's parents. Vanessa told the Precinct In-Charge – my parents are highly respected by the community. I gave my child to my parents this morning to look after her because I was not feeling well. I want to see my parents right now. I want my daughter right now, right here. Please bring them here. She was demanding justice to the Precinct in-charge.

Precinct-in-charge heard Vanessa and said – please wait here, let me go to arraignment area and find out about this case. Please be patient, I shall be back soon. He left the office for the downstairs to the booking area. When he went to downstairs, he could not believe himself to see what was happening to a very respectable member of the community, a physician, named Dr. George who was Palumbo family's personal physician. To put him in such a situation was nothing but a crime, Mr. Palumbo immediately apologized to Dr. George and wanted to know who has arrested Dr. George and his wife. Then he turned to Dr. George and said – Dr. George, I am truly sorry and ashamed that my officers put you through such an ordeal, I honestly believe that no apology can compensate the suffering you have been through, yet as an in-charge of the precinct I beg you to pardon these officers. Then he said – I am begging your forgiveness with my folded hands which you have taught me one day in your office.

Dr. George graciously accepted the apology and told – John,

I would request you to train your Officers so that they become polite, humble and more respectful and listen to the suspect what he has to say. You are my old friend, we spent so many years with one another, I cannot forget those old days. Then they had a short conversation about their families. Mr. Palumbo said to George – please come to my office, your daughter is waiting there for you. George and Grace took Melissa and followed Mr. Palumbo to his Office. George and Grace saw Vanessa, Pat and Pat's parents were waiting for them in the office. Vanessa jumped off her chair and came to her parents and said – mom, dad are you okay? I am very sorry that you had such a horrible experience to take care of my baby. Please forgive me. She embraced her parents tight. In the meantime Pat picked up Melissa and embraced her and told – let us go home we shall play any game whatever you want us to play. Melissa said – daddy, the police stopped grandpa, he won't listen to grandpa. He is not good. She gave her innocent opinion. Everyone heard her opinion. Mr. John Palumbo told to Melissa – nobody will stop your grandpa anymore, I will make sure of that. He kissed her affectionately. George said– John, I think we shall leave now. At least for this ugly incident we met once again. He looked at his family and said – let us go and let these gentlemen do their work. Mr. Palumbo said – you are right about that. All of them were happy at that moment. For George and Grace, it was a sigh of relief.

Pat's father, an ex-policeman said – Mr. Palumbo, with your permission I would like to see the arresting officer and speak to him for a minute. As an ex-policeman I want to say a few words to him.

Mr. Palumbo said – sure, you can speak to him. Then he called the arresting officer. Arresting Officer came to the office and said to Mr. Palumbo – sir, I am here to see you. He stood in front of all of them. Mr. Palumbo said to him – Mr. Owen is an ex-police man, he wants to talk to you for a minute. He introduced Mr. Owen to the arresting officer. They shook hands and then Mr. Owen said to the officer – you are here to protect people. I was in your shoes for many years. Dr. George is my in-law, my son's father-in-law. Underneath their brown skin same red color blood is flowing in them as yours and mine. Beside the skin color we are all the same. Never treat anyone with prejudice. You are here to serve the public, never be a reason for their sufferance. Always listen to the public, listen to what they want to say, be humble and courteous to them, if you do that, you will win their heart and they will love you. In my granddaughter my blood is flowing, Dr. George's blood is flowing, our grandchild is the living proof of unique harmony, love and affection of different human beings. She is carrying the blood of union of East and West. Remember – blood is always red, does not matter whose it is, please try to respect it. Then you will become a true policeman, a servant of humanity. Please remember this and I wish you all the best in your life. After finishing his words he turned to George and said – let us go now.

The Officer turned to Dr. George and Grace and told – I am truly ashamed of myself for treating you so poorly. Please forgive me, I shall always try to teach myself to rise above the prejudice and become a real Officer who will become a true servant of public and God. He turned to Grace and said – you are like my mother, I did not treat you like my mother, please punish me as a mother who punishes her child when they do not do right thing. His eyes were tearful, tears flowing through his cheeks. Grace could not see him crying, she hugged him and said – do not cry, your repentance will teach you the right from the wrong. Do visit us sometimes when you have a day off. I shall pray to God for the happiness of your life. Then she stopped and said – let us go home. All of them started to say good bye to Mr. Palumbo and started to leave for the home.

HOPE AGAINST LIVING IN FEAR

—

As of Oct 20, 2020, CORONAVIRUS CASES IN USA ARE GIVEN BELOW

Total Coronavirus Cases:
8.26 Million
Deaths:
220K

By this time all of us know what Coronavirus is and what harm it is doing to our human life, yet I thought it would be a good idea to write a few words about this virus, like it got its name etc. a very short description about it.

Coronaviruses derive their name from the fact that under electron microscopic examination, each virion is surrounded by a "corona," or halo. In Latin "Corona" means "Crown" and as it looks under the microscope like a crown, that is how it got the name "Coronavirus".

They are both the same thing but a **virion** is a **virus** that left the host cell and has fully matured to the ability to infect other cells. **Virus** is a general term for any kind of **virus** but **virions** are like adult **viruses** that are the outcome of an infected cell. **Virion** is a more specific term, for a **virus** particle.

Nearly 8.26 million peoples have been infected and death toll rose more than 220K (death rate is nearly 2.70% and recovery rate is 30.00% approximately.)

China informed the WHO of UNO that Coronavirus Covid-19 has spread in Wuhan City in China. They delayed to inform the WHO, intentional or innocent delay caused an increase of the infected peoples by a tremendous number and by the middle of January, 2020 many countries like Italy, USA and many others have experienced a huge increase in infections leading to death, by April 12, 2020 USA has lost 20637 lives in this Pandemic. Since it was delayed to inform most of the nations could not figure out how to handle this grave situation which caused death of so many peoples, eventually NIH of USA led by Dr. A. Fauci and his team found out certain clinical procedures and a few behavioral modification could put a break in spreading the disease effectively and these effective measures were recommended to protect its citizens. Some of them are social distance, using a face mask and washing hands very frequently with any soap for at least 20 seconds and dry the hands with dry paper towels.

We have read in history about the plague arrived in Europe in 1347 when 12 ships arrived from Black Sea and docked in Sicilian Port of Messina. As a result, this epidemic wiped out about 350 to 375 million people worldwide in 14th century. After that plague arrived in different part of the world and killed many peoples. The most recent attack of this disease was seen in Surat of Gujrat in India in 1994, as a result of this Pneumonic Plague epidemic many peoples died in that State. Now a new Pandemic arrived in the arena of humanity and its deadly force is felt in the whole globe and it has been named as Coronavirus. Besides killing of many lives, it has already created a major impact in our live in the USA. Besides loss of life this virus has created an unprecedented impact in the Socio-economic field of our life in USA.

In the wake of this Pandemic time the government officials have taken extraordinary measures to keep its citizens safe and well. Government is doing its job very well to keep us safe and well. We, the citizens of this country, should also join this war to stop this ominous deluge of Covid-19 Pandemic, we should follow instructions of the government agencies and their official leaders. As a good citizen I am personally following all the advice given by the authorities but it is not easy, since now I have enough time in my hands, I am trying to ponder over the situation we are in now, the effect of this deadly disease.

I am being self-quarantined for approximately last 64 days; I have plenty of time for self-scrutiny and assertion about the critical situation we are in. It is not only me and my family, thousands of families are in the same shoe as it is getting tighter and tighter. I have some personal experience of epidemic condition caused by cholera and small pox in the small village where I grew up as a teen ager, I have seen how everybody was coping with the situation when every day two three patients were dying, soon the village became a nightmare for the villagers, villagers were noticing everyday their loved ones were dying out of that epidemic. Everyone was scared to death and the epidemic continued for at least next six months. This happened when I was a teenager, but in this Pandemic, I am a retired matured adult and I have a family to look after, life is more complicated than before, needs of life are many now but ways to fulfill them are very limited, so everyone like me at this time is at a loss what to do.

In the wake of this Pandemic life has become more complex, society is in jeopardy and life is in danger, Government is in dilemma how to protect the citizens, how to stop this Pandemic, but this is a very difficult task, all of us need to be together to fight this monster and make this country safer and make the life normal again.

We the people of this country have to stand by the government to stop this Pandemic but as an individual our strength is very limited, so we must unite together and must sacrifice our living standard until we overcome this difficulty. These difficulties will come from every angle of life and we have to cope with those and ultimately someday this nightmare will be over for all of us.

Many of us migrated to this country for a better life, we struggled and worked hard for many years and finally our families became stable financially, some of us are retired and enjoying the retired life. Financial stability gave us hope for the best. Now due to this Coronavirus Pandemic the stock market is plummeting, peoples' savings are depleting to a great extent, savings are vanishing, everybody is scared about the future financial trouble. Now many of us believe that our financial stability is vaporized, our happiness is on the verge of disappearing. Social life is almost gone, we cannot go out, we have to maintain social distance, and we have to use facial masks to protect ourselves so that we do not get infected by this deadly disease. Socialization with friends and family has become an event of the past, friends cannot visit friends, family cannot meet families anymore, and grandparents cannot have grandchildren in home anymore, loving relationship has disappeared, fear of getting the infection of Coronavirus has surpassed, all the joys of companionship and relationship are virtually nonexistent, our lives are practically on the edge of a cliff, about to fall and crash any time soon.

Millions of peoples are out of work. Small businesses employ about 70% percent of work force. Restaurants, small stores, grocery stores, salons, barber shops and many other small service stores are closed by the order of the government. The impact of this closure is observed in many folds, namely no haircut, no nail cutting, and even no hamburger from the McDonald. We, the Americans, experienced this kind of stalemate of life when 911 terrorist act took place in the year 2001. That was done by some Islamic religious terrorists, three thousand plus persons lost their lives but this Coronavirus has already claimed more than twenty-two thousand lives. Nobody knows whose turn is coming when, a sharp sword of Coronavirus is hanging over our head, it is only matter of time when it is coming down on someone's neck and cut the head off. Life is under the current of panic and fear. It does not end here. It is coming from all directions, north, south, east or west, the whole country is in danger.

Once the Coronavirus is contained, the impact of this pandemic will still be far reaching in the society. Now most of the big companies are letting their employees to work from home via computers. Employees are very happy in this time because they can work from home and getting their salaries as well. This is the good news for both employer and employee, a real harmonious relation between the owner and the employee. Now, everyone in employment force is working hard from home to keep his job and as a result the production is way above the normal time, more accurately now one employee is producing more than time and half of normal time. So, employer is getting three employees work done by two employees, the employers will figure it out very soon and once this Pandemic is over, they will reduce their workforce accordingly, as result a good number of people will lose their jobs and eventually become unemployed.

One of the worst effects of this virus is that our children cannot go to school or playground as a result they are not getting face to face teachings in school, since they cannot go to playground, they cannot get any physical exercises either, this may definitely cause obesity in some of the children. Some adults who are physically active face the same situation, they cannot go to Gym, or who play tennis or golf, they cannot do that either, they are not getting their exercises which may lead to diabetes, obesity or heart related complications, overall, the consequence may be a rise in health-related issue for all of us. It has been determined that obesity is also a grave risk factor for the infection of Coronavirus Pandemic.

The other side of the coin is even worse. During this

mandatory staying home among young married couples may give rise to some marital problem. Normally each married couple spends about seven hours together besides the sleeping time, calculation is like this, out of twenty-four hours if you take out twelve hours for work related use including commuting time, then remaining twelve hours are for sleep and home related activities. As a result now a days husband and wife has more time for interactions, for difference of opinions, for small altercations which may turn into a big one, small drops of water makes an ocean, this ocean can also be wild, similarly staying together may also create huge commotion and eventually divorce filing may take place, also some of them will be victims of depression and other mental issues, these may also add fuel to fire of addiction of alcohol or drugs, even though when Coronavirus will be contained, these social issues will burn our society little by little like a slow fire of husk. Our ephemeral memory became very feeble that we have forgot that after 911, we could never put our lives together, quality of life never came back at all to its previous satisfactory stage, on the other hand our daily life is now circling around security line etc. for any flights or any big play or sports event and it has become part of life, we like it or not, we are just in it and we shall never be able to come out this menace.

Similarly, someday our scientists will discover some vaccine for Covid-19, may be, they will also find out some specific drug to treat the severe symptoms of this disease but it will never be eradicated from the environment, it will float around the air all over the world round the year. Seasons will come when this virus will infect peoples again but its morbidity will prevail but mortality may not be as bad as now, it may even be a seasonal disease like flu or any other disease which spreads during certain time of the year.

The use of drugs like Chloroquine and Hydroxychloroquine for prophylaxis of Covid-19 may give serious side effects for their use, symptoms of heart disease, liver disease may appear and a certain number of patients who are suffering and treated with these drugs may suffer again from such conditions of side effects.

So, according to many experts it may be contained now but it will never be eradicated completely, it is here and like it or not, it is going to stay here forever as one of the deadliest maladies of all time. Covid-19 Pandemic will ameliorate someday but the devastating effect of it will be remembered for many years to come.

It feels that we are all imprisoned in a jail where thousands of wild and hungry animals in the form of Coronavirus are running around to whet their appetites and we are only waiting to be attacked by those hungry ferocious animals. We have no recourse to a safe situation, rather we are only waiting to become victims and help this Covid-19 to whet their thirst and hunger by becoming their prey. For now, it looks like that our life is on the razor thin edge of this Covid-19. This angst is not going to end soon, this Covid-19 will scintillate so many deaths in our country we, the citizens of this country will be punctilious and do whatever it needs to create the situation of eradication of the Covid-19 from this country.

Among all these Pandemic detrimental effects where thousands of families are suffering from its deadly attacks, I kept receiving phone calls from my friends every day that they heard their known peoples are being infected by this deadly malady.

About seven or eight persons whom I know very closely have been infected with this Covi-19. Some of them are my friends. One of these friends is Amal Das. He is in his late forties with good health. He is an athlete who loves to walk and run, in fact he runs 5 miles every day. When I heard a healthy person like him has been infected by Coronavirus, I was very worried for him but could not do anything, I could not go to hospital to visit him, I felt very helpless and started to pray to my God for his recovery. Two or three weeks later I received a phone call from Amal and I was relieved and very happy to hear his voice. He described the pain and agony of sufferings which he had gone through and said "I would not like my worst enemy to go through this pain and sufferings". Then he sent me a video clip for one minute in which he was trying to breath while doing breathing exercise. He mentioned that the nurse made the recording for him. When my wife and I watched the video, we realized the degree of sufferance these patients go through. It was a sheer learning experience for us about the severity of this malady called Coronavirus. We were relieved that Amal recovered fully and started his normal life again. Also, one of my friend's mother-in-law became sick with Coronavirus and did not survive, she waw 79 years old.

I received a very scary telephone call from one of my good friends of India that his son, a thirty- seven-year-old brilliant scholar is sick with Covid-19. This young man stood first Math

Olympiad of India and he came to Houston University to study his Masters and Ph D. Since his father and I were good friends he came to New York and stayed with us for a few days before he joined his university. After that he visited us a few more times during his stay in USA. After his graduation he went back to India and joined a multinational company in a very high position. Even after moving to India he used call us two or three times in a year and always said "Uncle, I always talk about you and Auntie to my dad and mom. Whenever I visited you, you made my stay very comfortable and always treated as if I was your own child. I shall never forget your love and affection. Please remember you have to spend a few days with me and my wife in our home. Please reserve a few days for us in your travel period." So, when we heard this news, we were very sad and called his parents regularly. In the mean time were praying daily for his recovery in our daily prayer of God. Finally, the good news came that he has fully recovered from Covid-19 and resumed his normal activity, we had a sigh of relief and thanked our God for his recovery.

It is very disappointing for any human being to go through this ominous time and we have to find some way to cope with this time of struggling existence. Personally, I believe that this is the time that we resort to get help from our inner self, we should never lose our inner strength, and must depend on our spiritual strength, and we must submit ourselves to our almighty to get strength so that we can pass through this Pandemic day. Previously, whenever there was any problem in my life, I always sought answers from the holy book The

Shrimad Bhagavad Gita where Lord Krishna explained to Arjuna how to cope with life in any difficult situation like this. Actually, The Shrimad Bhagavad Gita enlightens everyone on how to cope up with various situations in life. It uses the conversation between Lord Krishna and Arjuna to highlight initial negative coping mechanisms exhibited by the latter. It goes on to showcase positive coping with skills suggested by Lord Krishna and implemented by Arjuna. The Bhagavad Gita, through this "case-based methodology," teaches us how to cope with a demanding situation like this one. We should never give up our hope and believe in that whatever happens for the very best, we have to believe in it. The spirit which we have in our heart will always nourish our hopes and will always keep us safe and well. If we always feel that some bad things are going to happen to us then this may lead to us to paranoia and we will become more fearful and panicky. In these situations, it is always better that we accept the situation and try to change it for better, we should learn the coping skills and adapt ourselves to come out of the importunity which may put us in more dire and fearful situation.

There are **195 countries** in the world. The United Nations (UN) recognizes **195** sovereign countries. 193 of these countries are members of the United Nations, and two - the Holy See and the State of Palestine - are simply observer states. By some definitions, there are 197 countries in the world. Out of all these countries the root cause of Pandemic points to China. It is the responsibility of all these countries to find and determine if China is really responsible for the spread of this epidemic, if it is determined that the rogue administration of China is found responsible for this Pandemic, then the United Nation should punish China for causing such a heinous act against humanity. Now it will be seen that the no-good UN has the intention and strength to punish China and its Leaders financially or by any other means so that none of the countries will ever resort to do this kind of detrimental act to the humanity.

We should prepare ourselves to acknowledge that the post Covid-19 life may be the same as the pre Covid-19 life. We have to understand that Covid-19 will leave a deep scar and fear in our daily life, like post 911 life may not be the same, changes may take place and we should accept this change gracefully.

Finally, it is very necessary that all of us start praying according to our faith and start to believe that this wild Coronavirus Pandemic will be tamed and the fear of this Coronavirus finally will be eradicated with the combined help of faith, coping skills and knowledge of medical science. Every night ends with light of the day. Similarly, we must be hopeful that now we have almost reached end of the tunnel and rays of light will appear soon. Despite the fact that fear of Coronavirus is very dominant but we must be strong and at the end of this our hope will always prevail, we will conquer the deadly effect of Pandemic and finally we will restore our lives to a new normalcy which will be enjoyed by every citizen of our country.

Note: 1. By the time it is published the numbers of death etc. will change

2. Used references from different sources of information

JOHNNY'S FAMILY

—

When I try to remember the Head Master (Head Sir), I always see the person wearing white Khaddar Dhoti and Punjabi, waiting in entrance of the School at 10:15 am in the morning and was asking every student "how are you?. Yes, he used to wear an eye glass also with a thick lens which probably meant that his eye sight was poor. When I saw him for the first time, I was very young, may be 11/12 year old boy. About the first meeting I shall describe later how I felt at that time. From now on I shall call him Head Sir as everyone in the school used to call him.

When I saw him for the first time, I did not know how old he was, as I imagine today after so many years, I think he was in his mid-thirties, very thin, tall, a little long nose but overall he was very attractive and pleasing, yet a fear always induced in us whenever we looked at him for any reason whatsoever. Lots of peoples used to come to see him during the school hours and everyone was automatically very respectful to him. His profound personality was always dominating in nature yet very likable at the end. Everybody liked him, students were afraid to speak to him, teachers were also afraid because he put the students first, he would not tolerate anytime any teacher would be harsh unnecessarily to any student, if it came to his notice, he would immediately ask the teacher to see him in his office and would tell them – please treat them with extreme love and care, they are our future of our country, help them educate with love and care, only then they will grow up as a decent human being who will care for his fellow human beings. The teacher would realize his mistake and understand the inner meaning of the words of Head Master and most of the times regret for their mistake and say- sorry sir, I shall try to remember your advice and treat them with love and affection. Conversation would end there and the teacher would go to his classroom happily. This was a normal manner how he administered his ideals of life with justice and respect. This was he who was our Head Sir, Anath Bandhu Bhattacharya an excellent teacher, guide and a philosopher.

Later on I came to know him really well. He used to live in a small refugee Colony near the school. He was married and his wife Neela was a very charming young woman who would always support her husband for better or worse. His house was a small hut made of bamboo pillars walls were made of combined long and thin bamboo branches, and the roof of the hut was nothing but clay tiles put in their sockets which hold them together. Later on I came to know that he was a victim of partition of India, all his family members were killed or missing during the heinous crime of atrocities against Hindus and Moslems. Division of India for the sake of Freedom was a historic mistake done by Gandhi and Jinnah the then political leaders of Congress Party and then Muslim League. Primarily a land for Muslims or Pakistan was the brain child of British Rulers supported by Md. Ali Jinnah. Eventually India was divided before freedom and leaders of Congress Party and Muslim League made the historic blunder of dividing a nation on the basis of religion. Hindus and Moslems lived peacefully for centuries together but once this division was created, hell of riots broke out, millions of peoples were killed in that heinous deluge of mayhem. Millions of peoples were displaced, lost their homes and belongings, Leaders of Congress and Muslim League became ministers of India and Pakistan, they did not care about the sufferings of common peoples, they were only interested to divide the country and obtain a no good freedom. Our Head Sir was one of those victims of division of the country was our Head Sir. Some of the members of his family were killed, some of them were missing since then, never found at all, he was the only survivor with his wife, eventually started to float like a straw in the river and eventually reached here and decided to live in this community. This community was totally built with the displaced peoples from East Pakistan, they found their way to establish a small school for their children but could not find a good teacher who could lead this newly established school, when they saw Head Sir, the neighbors became very happy and they informed about this man to their leader Balai Babu who also has also willingly donated his land for these destitute families and helped them a lot to build these houses with his own money and land. Balai Babu was a rich business man who owned a few tea gardens in Dooars area of North Bengal. When he heard about this man, he invited him and his wife to his home to have some lunch one day.

Balai Babu's real name is Balaichand Banerjee. He is a well know person in the town and his influence went a long way even to Central Government of Delhi. The Ministers of the State Government respected him a lot and they always revered him for his honesty and philanthropic activities. The place where he lived was a moderate house nobody would even imagine that the owner of this house is none other than the famous industrialist Mr. Balaichand Banerjee. The inside beauty of the house spectacular, this house he built in his early years, he loves to live in this house with his wife Sheila. When Anath and his wife Neela entered the foyer of the house, they both were astonished to see a spacious area, a beautiful chandelier hanging from the roof, a beautiful sofa set is resting on a small colorful carpet, in front of the sofa set a mahogany made coffee table is sitting to add the beauty of the room, seeing all these things Neela said – Masterjee, what a beautiful house, I have never seen any house like this, so beautiful, before she could finish her words, Sheila and her husband Balai Babu came and greeted them, asked them to sit on the couch and both of them sat on the chairs in front of the couch. Neela and Antath both touched the feet of Sheila and Balai Babu and expressed their respect to them and sat down on the couch which Neela admired to be very beautiful. And Neela looked at Sheila and said – auntie, your house is very beautiful, for the first time I am in a house like this. She was really overwhelmed by the inside beauty of the house. She was happy.

Auntie Sheila looked at happy Neela and said – Neela, we are very happy to see that two you have come to our house today. First take these snacks and then we shall talk for as long as you want. Then she looked at one of her household helps and said – go, bring the snacks and give them. The help came back in a very short time and put the foods on the table. The other help came with some drinks and put the glasses on the same table. At this time Sheila looked at Anath and said – please take some food first then talk to your uncle. Sheila noticed that Anath and Neela are not taking non vegetarian item, they were eating only vegetarian items. Noticing this Sheila said – take some fish fry and freshly prepared lamb Kabab.

Anath felt little embarrassed to confess, looked at Sheila and said – we do not eat any fish or meat. We are followers of Lord Krishna and Radha.

At this time Balai Babu got surprised and said – really, you two are also Vaishnavas, very glad to hear it, our house is a home for Lord Krishna and Radha. Now, this is an extra reason for us to become more exulted to see you guys in our house. Then he looked at Anath and said – let us leave these ladies alone. Let us go and sit down in the Lawn and speak.

Then he showed the path towards the backyard of the house and Anath started to follow him. Backyard is surrounded by high wall and beautiful rose plants were all around, few merry tulips and other flowers which Anath did not know. In the middle of the yard is a big garden umbrella, under which is a fiber glass table and six chairs, on the top of the table there is jug of water and six glasses, may be they always have six guests for this table, Anath thought. He liked the respectful hospitality which Balai Babu is showing to them. This man is very rich yet so humble that Anath has already made up his mind, if he is offered the job he will accept it. Both of them sat on the chair facing each other so that they could converse face to face. Balai Babu said to his help – please give us some tea.

Anath said – sir, I do not drink tea or coffee, please forgive me.

Balai Babu insisted – this is from my garden, it tastes really well and quality of this tea is very good and to me it tastes like heavenly delicious. Please try, I insist.

Anath looked into Balai Babu's eyes and said – sir, I do not want to disrespect you, please ask him to bring for me also.

Balai Babu looked into his watch and said – President of the School will arrive soon, once he is here we shall start to speak about the school. At this time a gentleman showed up and with folded hands, he expressed his regards to both of them and said – I hope, I am not late. Then he sat in one of those chairs and looked at Anath and said- I hope you are comfortable here. This is my second home, Balai Babu and Boudi always are very well known for their hospitality and caring for everyone. These two peoples are very close to heart, once you stay here, you will see that I did exaggerate a bit. Then he looked at Balai Babu and said -, let us start our meeting, hopefully we would be able to convince this young man to join our school.

At this time Balai Babu looked at Anath and said – Masterjee, please tell a few words about yourself, we want to hear from you.

Anath looked at both them and said – as you have heard that we like this place and I am looking for a job as a teacher but first I would like to know about your school and students, I have already understood the kindness you have already shown to us but I also want to see if I am the right person whom you are looking for.

The newly arrived man said – my name is Anil Roy and I am the President of the school and Balai Babu is the Secretary of the school. Balai Babu has donated the land for the school and he has also built the school house, it has adequate space for the class rooms but we do not have enough students to fill the class rooms because it is a very new school, only one and half year old and we did not find a real leader who can lead the school to a higher level so that more parents want to admit their children into this school and eventually the school's reputation will attract the students. We are looking to have a Head Master for this school and this Head Master would take the full responsibility for making it a great school.

Balai Babu added – once we get more students with your leadership everything will fall in its place and you won't have to regret that you joined this school. Now if you say a few words about your education and experience, we would like to hear about that.

Anath looked at both of them and said – I received first class in M.A. in English also have a B.T. degree in Teaching and I received first class also in B.T. After passing the degrees I went back to my village where my family lived for many years. My father established a school for the local children and I joined their as a Head Master. I worked hard for that school and in five years we could make that school where everyone wanted to put their children for their education. Before children had to walk four miles for a high school, not anymore, this school could provide the students of nearby villages for their perfect education. Bye the by I want to let you know that when I passed my master's, I was offered a job in the college where I studied my B.A honors in English but I did not accept that offer because I always wanted to become a school teacher who would educate the children and convert them to better human beings who in turn would build a nation of excellent citizens, I dream a nation who would excel in every aspect of life. In this context I want to mention that higher education is not meant for every student, however, every student has different talent by which they can do excellent in life, someone may not be good in scholastic education but he might have business talent by which he can become a very successful member of the society, some may be gifted with art, school's job, I believe, should inculcate the thirst for his artwork so that he can flourish to the fullest extent of his talent, School's job is to prepare a student for his own talent, not to create a finished product of general standard, I want my students to succeed in their lives to their fullest potential. This is the main reason why I have decided to become a school teacher. I know, I could always become a civil servant, professor or any officer but I decided to dedicate my life for the sake of students, the future of our country, when I see that one of students joins army, police or any university, I feel very proud that they all have one thing in common, my early teachings of their lives, I feel very happy to see them, my old students. My dream – I want to create a society of real human beings who will dedicate their lives for the benefit of the society. His sincerity and dedication made Balai Babu and Anil spellbound, they were moved with this man's ideal and dream. He articulated his points very well.

Anil and Balai Babu were very impressed with Anath's speech and both of them felt that he is the right person for their school. Both of them decided to hire Anath as their next Head Master.

Balai Babu told – Anath, both of us feel that if you take the responsibility of our school and the students, we shall try our best to take care of you and your wife. Now, you tell us what you want from the school as your salary and benefits. We want to hear from you.

Anath smiled and said – sir, we are two in the family, our need is very small, all I want is a small place to live and some money with which we can buy some food and clothes, that's all I need for us. I need one other thing, the freedom with which I can run the daily activities of the school, if I get that I promise, I shall see the end of the sky to fulfill your dreams to make your school a real institution which will create real human beings who will be the wealth of the human society and the country as well.

Balai Babu and Anil listened to his every word, saw the dreams in his eyes, felt the dedication of his heart and said – I have a small piece of land, and a very small hut which has three rooms, it is about five minutes' walk from the school and I am going to build a brick house in that place for the Head Master as soon as possible so that you two can build your nest with happiness. This land and house comes with this position of Head Master of the school, this was the idea in my mind for a long time, I am very happy that you are going to get it, I shall register the land and the building in your name as soon as the building is constructed, may be the whole process will take about next five or six months.

The new would be Head Master Anath heard everything Balai Babu said and then he said – sir, thank you very much for offering the job, I shall take the job but I cannot accept the land and the building from you. Sorry sir, I am not trying to be disrespectful to you both, but my heart does not support that I take anything for which I did not work. If you sell me it to me at the market price and if I can afford the market price only then I shall purchase them, however I shall have to pay you in monthly instalment, please take the payment from my salary every month. This is my entreaty to you both. I do not want to own anything which I did not earn. You do not have to let your decision know now, however I shall take the job with or without the proposal of buying the land and the house.

Anil and Balai Babu were at a loss hearing his decision about the land and the house. Honesty and determination of Anath made them perplexed, they did not know what to say but one thing they were very happy about this Head Master is that he is a person of infinite honesty. They realized this young man is very honest and whatever he is, he is not greedy, frankly to find a person like him was really hard and scarce. So both of them agreed to his proposal and offered him the school and the house and the land. Balai Babu being a businessman knew that they have found the real gem for their students and the school as well. Both of them told him – we agree with your proposal and we are very happy to get you as our Head Master. Now this was the story of one side, the other side was yet to be revealed.

That side came to everyone's notice when Neela and Balai Babu's wife Sheila came back smiling to the backyard where all three men were discussing about the school. Neela and Sheila sat on the table and Sheila said – "Neela and I went to our temple to pray to our God Radha Krishna. Neela adorned our God with flower and she sang a beautiful Bhajan, I am astonished to hear her melodious voice and her skill of voice told me that she used to practice music daily and she is a real great singer. I requested her if she can sing in front of our deity when we celebrate the "Dol Purnima" and she agreed to help us on that celebration day. I request to both of you that please hire Anath for our school. These two will make our community a better place to live."

Since that day Anath became the Head Master of the School and Neela became the most favorite person of Sheila and Neela started to call her "Kakima". These strengthened their family bond and mutual respect for each other. These two families came together in every respect of their lives. Eventually Neela gave birth to baby girl, both families took this child as the gift of God, "Radha Krishna". Time flies fast, it went fast for them also, Head Master turned the school to a very high quality school and families are turning to this school to educate their children, the ineffable aroma of fame of the school and Head Master rose in the sky and flew in vicinal small towns and some of other schools of those towns wanted to allure the Head Master to join their schools for a far more better salary and benefits but Anath refused those offers very politely, Neela and Anath loved this community and family of Balai Babu, they could not even imagine to live in any other place than this beloved community. Losing the family and friends once due to the effects of the horrific and detrimental atrocities of riots during the freedom of India, Anath and Neela did not want to go through the same path of agony and pain of losing friends and families, once is enough for them.

A few years later one day Balai Babu was coming back home from his office, his driver stopped the car on a traffic light. At that time a little boy approached to the driver and asked – can I clean your car? He had a piece of cloth in his hand. He started to clean the side view mirrors of the car. At that time the driver told the little boy – stop cleaning, I clean the car myself. The light became green and the driver started to roll. During this conversation Balai Babu was busy reading a file from the office. This type of incident is not new, rather very frequently he witnesses these destitute little boys, his heart goes out to them but cannot help them, nor the driver pays any attention to these unfortunate poor boys, he feels bad at that time, then he forgets these incidents, he feels bad but life goes on. Balai Babu felt something special about this little, he felt this boy may become someone, should he get a chance in his life. He sometimes speaks to his wife Sheila and expresses his anger towards the leaders of the country for the corruption and injustice which prevailed in the nation. For next few days this little boy was not seen in the same corner of the same traffic light. Balai Babu forgot about this little boy, then one day he saw the boy again in the same place. This time he told the driver – pull the car on the side and call this little boy who wanted to clean the car. Ask him to clean the car.

The little boy came and started to clean, he was giving his best effort to shine the color of the car with his little hand, and Balai Babu noticed that. He put his hard work for next fifteen twenty minutes and then said – Babu, on certain spots it should be more shining, but I could not remove those spots for some reason. If you pass this way tomorrow, I shall definitely put some more cream and rub on those spots, I have finished all my creams today. Balai Babu asked – how much is the cleaning cost, tell the price. Balai Babu looked the little boy to get his response. The little boy looked at Balai Babu and said – Bapuji, I could not complete the job right, I do not think that you should pay me. I do not want any money from you today. When I polish your car real good tomorrow I shall ask you to pay me. I cannot accept any price for the unfinished job. Then he started to walkaway form the car.

Balai Babu at that time told him – don't go, what is your name? He offered him a five rupee note.

The little boy looked at Balai Babu respectfully and said – Bapuji, I told you I cannot accept any price for it, this will be dishonest of me, please do not ask me to become a dishonest person, my name is Johnny Jacob.

Balai Babu asked the boy – where are your parents? Where do you live?

The boy replied – Bapuji, my parents passed away. My father

was killed in the riot and my mother passed away one year ago. Now, I live in the other side of the colony with a man whom I call him uncle, he is not my real uncle, since I am an orphan he became kind enough to give me a shelter in his place. He always keeps an eye on my wellbeing. My uncle is also very poor, we live in a slam on the other side of the town.

What happened to your mother? How did she die? – Balai Babu asked Johnny.

My mother had a diarrhea, she went to hospital but nobody took care of her. Everyone wanted money from my mother, she did not have any money, since she could not pay and she died in the hospital untreated. I lost my mother and became alone in the whole world. Thank God, the uncle took me in with him. But he does not have any money, I have to work for a living that is the reason why I clean cars every day to make some money.

Balai Babu felt his heart is getting heavy hearing this little boy's sad story of losing parents and eventually became an orphan. But the boy is very brave and facing the hardship of life with full honesty and dignity which lots of adults do not even possess these day. He looked at the boy and said – Johnny, see me tomorrow here, and remember you did not finish the job.

Johnny smilingly replied – sure, Bapuji, I shall be here to clean your car and I shall do a fabulous job, you will see tomorrow. Please give me permission to leave now. Balai Babu saw an undaunted little boy walking to get ready for next day's battle against hunger and poverty. This little boy's punctilious and ataraxic behavior made an impression in Balai Babu.

Normally Balai Babu always sits down with his wife Sheila

for a cup of tea after returning from work. This day was not different either, he sat with his wife and said – Sheila, a strange thing happened today, I met a little boy who came to my car and asked the driver to clean the car. He cleaned the car but could not do it up to his satisfaction, so he would not take the money from me. This little boy is very honest and hard working. He lost both of his parents, he lives with a person who has given him shelter and this man also does not have a good job, so this little boy has to work. I wish, someone would give him a chance in his life so that someday he grew up like a real successful human being.

Sheila listened to Balai Babu's description about this little boy, she felt sorry about this boy and said – Do you know the name of this boy? If you feel this boy can turn around his life with some help, then why don't you do that? May be we should bring the boy in our house and let him stay with us. Ask him tomorrow if he wants to work in our home, if he does, bring him in our home. We shall keep him here.

Balai Babu listened to his wife and said – let me see if I see him tomorrow, then I shall ask him to come to our home and stay with us. Anyway, we will find out about it tomorrow. Sheila, please give me a cup of coffee.

Sheila looked at her husband with deceitful anger and said – now a days you are drinking too much coffee, you have to be careful, your heart is not good, from tomorrow you will drink coffee two times only, once in the morning and once when you come back from the office. She was firm in her voice.

"Yes my darling, no more coffee from tomorrow" – was Balai

Babu's short reply. This conversation ended here between them. Sheila said – let me go and put Radha and Krishna in their bed of temple. This was their daily routine to worship Radha and Krishna by offering five lighted lamps and some food. But for last few years the status of this prayer has been augmented to a new divine altar by dint of Neola's live musical performance to the God.

Although Balai Babu expected to see the little boy Johnny next day but to his dire disappointment, he did not see him next few days, everyday his expectation was going up and up for seeing that little boy but unfortunately that little boy did not show up at all for nest fest few days. Finally, Balai Babu and Sheila gave up hope of seeing him and stopped discussing about the little boy Johnny Jacob. The little boy Johnny did not come in their mind or discussion at all for next two weeks.

Johnny Jacob felt little better today. He was suffering from stomach disease with fever for last few days. Nobody was around to help him. He could not get up, felt feeble and hungry yet did not find anyone to fetch him some food. So, he did what any normal person would do, he got up and started to walk towards the shopping area where he could buy some food to whet his appetite. He reached the neighborhood restaurant and sat down on a chair. He started to look at the menu and found out that this place was too expensive for him. He brought out the money from his pocket and counted them. This money he saved by working for weeks, now he has to spend it for just one meal, he could not agree with that, so he decided to go to some other cheaper place. In the meantime, the waiter came to him and put a glass of water on the table and asked him – what can I bring for you? Please let me know.

Johnny stood up said – sorry, your place is too expensive for me, I cannot afford anything here, I have to find a cheaper place. Do you know any place nearby where I can get some cheap food? He started to walk out.

The waiter told him – there is another place near our restaurant, once you get out of the restaurant go to your right, you will find that place where their food is by far cheaper than here.

Johnny found the cheaper restaurant and filled his stomach to his content and he did not had to spend that much money either. Once hunger disappeared he started to think about last few days. He could not get up and go to his work. He felt very bad thinking about that he could not keep his promise that he would clean Bapuji's car in the next day. He thought Balai Babu must have thought bad things about him since he could not shine the car next day. So, he decided to go back home and pick up his stuff which are required for his cleaning job. He did not want Bapuji think that he was a dishonest person, by all means he always tried to remain honest, sincere and hard working. While these things were in his mind he did not know when he came to the same traffic light with a hope that he would meet Bapuji in the same place. He kept an eye on all the oncoming cars so that he could see Bapuji and the car. Finally he saw Bapuji and asked the driver to stop, Bapuji also saw him and asked his driver to stop. The car stopped on the side of the street and this time Bapuji came out of the car and said - Johnny, what happened, you did not show up, are you alright? He looked at

Johnny and it seemed to him that this little boy looked thin and his sunken pale eyes and his sunken cheeks let Balai Babu know that this little boy was definitely ill for last few days.

The little boy said – Bapuji, please forgive me for not coming to clean and shine your car that day because I was very ill and could not get up from the bed. I am recovered now and today I am going to finish the job which I left unfinished the other day. Then he took out the cream, foam and rubbing brush etc. to start his job. Balai Babu kept watching while he was working on his car. The boy started to sweat heavily because he was rubbing the surface of the car very hard to make it as shiny as possible. After watching that the boy was really trying very hard, Balai Babu said – Johnny, it looks good, it is shining, and you can stop now and get your money.

Johnny said – Bapuji, I took some time already but please give me two more minutes, let me just finish this spot and the car will look all shiny and beautiful. He finished rubbing and said – Bapuji, look at the car, she looks so shinny and beautiful. Then looked at Balai Babu with a smiling face, he felt proud of his job.

Balai Babu looked at the car and said – Johnny, very good, job well done. Now take your money and he offered him a five rupee note.

Johnny took the money and said – please give me two rupees only, I get two rupees from every of my customers. I cannot and should not charge you more. If you have change, please give me two rupees, if you do not have change now, please pay me later.

Balai Babu realized the mind of this kid and paid him two

rupees and said – can you see me tomorrow in my home? This is my address, he handed over the address to him and said – don't forget to come to my home tomorrow, make sure you come with your uncle, then told the driver to start for home,

Balai Babu came home and sat with his wife and said – Sheila, the little boy came today, he could not meet me because he was sick with some stomach ailment. He cleaned the car very good and the car looks very fine. I told him to come to our home tomorrow with his uncle who took him after his mother passed away.

Next morning Johnny came to Balai Babu's home with his uncle. Some of helps asked them to sit on couch but they were standing anyway. Johnny was looking around and was astonished to see that some people could have house who beautiful, he had never seen in his life, he was totally mesmerized with beauty of the house and expensive furniture which were in the room where they were standing. At this time Balai Babu came in the room with his wife, Sheila. They sat down and asked Johnny and his uncle to sit down also. Johnny and his uncle started to sit on the floor, at that time Balai Babu held their hands and asked them to sit on the chairs. Both of them sat on the chair but they looked very shy and uncomfortable. At that time Balai Babu said to both of them – be normal and comfortable, feel free and normal, you have come to our house, do not be shy. At this time one of the helps came with some breakfast and put the food on the breakfast table. Sheila and her husband sat on one side of the table and then asked Johnny and his uncle to sit on the other side of the table. But both of them were very hesitant to sit there, they were trying to sit on the floor again but Balai Babu asked both of them very politely to sit next to them. Both of them sat with great hesitation and started to eat the food very silently. Johnny's uncle was a very thin person, his eyes were pale and he was dressed in old and torn clothes. Everything told that this person was very poor. During the breakfast Balai Babu asked Johnny – we want you to live with us from now, and Johnny looked at his uncle, before he could say anything his uncle promptly said – sir, I think that would be very good for Johnny, he would not have to work hard in the sun, at least he would get some good food every day. Please keep him, Sir. This poor child lost his father and mother in such a way that he had no place to go, seeing that I thought, let him stay with me, I could not let him to wonder as flaneur in the streets of the town. It would be a heaven for this young child. Then looked at Johnny and said – you stay here with Sir from now. I shall bring back your remaining clothes from the home tomorrow. It will be good for your life, if you ever want to see me, you can always come to my place any time. Always be obsequious and listen to Sir and Mataji mother). Always take good care of them, remember, they became so kind to you never ever let them down by your behavior.

Possibly this was Johnny's destiny that his life disembogue around the life of Balai Babu and Sheila, a wealthy family of this small town. It was God's will that this child would receive the blessings of this family, family of Balai Babu and Sheila.

About a month later Sheila and Balai Babu were having tea in their back yard and Johnny was working nearby with flower plants. Sheila said – Johnny is very attentive to whatever he is asked to do, he finishes it very neatly. His sense of responsibility, duty and sincerity are above any question, God bless him all his life. Then Sheila said – I should let you know that whenever he goes to stores, he makes a list with cost and gives me the account how much he paid and how much money came back. And he writes them very neatly. His hand writing is very neat and beautiful, I was astonished to see such beautiful hand writing. She finished her talk and showed the receipt he made for the shopping which he did in the morning today. Balai Babu looked and was also surprised immensely to his mind. He called Johnny, showed him the Johnny's hand written paper and said – Is this your hand writing?

Johnny replied – yes Bapuji, I have written this account to show exactly how much I spent and how much money came back, this way Mataji will know exactly how much I paid for each item, that is why I have written this chit.

Balai Babu listened to him and said – how did you learn to write, did you attend any school?

"My mother taught me to read and write, then she admitted me into a school where I studied up to class six, then suddenly my mother passed away and my school days came to an end because I could not pay the fees of the school, I wish my mother was alive and I could go to school. I have buried my schooling when I buried my mother in her grave – said Johnny. His voice told that he was very sad to tell this story to Balai Babu.

Listening to Johnny's story Balai Babu felt very sad in his

mind for this unfortunate boy. He looked at Johnny and said – do you remember the name of the school?

Johnny mentioned the name of the school to his Bapuji and his Bapuji asked him – if you get a chance would you like to go to school again?

Johnny replied – yes Bapuji. His eyes were glittering with hope. He just remembered that his mother always used to tell him – son, study hard, make it your Mantra, and get a good education, only that will give you a good respectable life in future. Thinking about his mother's advice Johnny felt his eyes were getting watery. He felt that the dawn of his life has arrived in his doorstep again.

Next day Balai Babu called the school which Johnny attended and spoke to the Head Master. The Head Master informed him that Johnny took the annual examination of 6th grade and after that he did not go back to his school. He did not even go back to get the results of his final examination either. Bye the by the Head Master informed Balai Babu that Johnny stood first in his class in the annual examination. Also mentioned that Johnny was a meritorious student. He wished that Johnny did not leave the school, with Johnny's result his school could have been famous in this area.

Few weeks later, Balai Babu went to the Head Master Anath with Johnny. Seeing them the Head Master told – Balai Babu, you could call me, I could come to your home and see you.

Balai Babu smiled and said – this time it is necessary that I come to you. I want you to admit Johnny into your school. Year before last he finished grade 6 and stood first in his class.

Since his mother passed away he did not go to school because he did not have any money. Sheila and I noticed that this child is very smart, so we decided to send him to school, meaning your school. Now, please find out in which class he should be admitted into.

Head Master said – sir, this is very good news. I also thought Johnny is a smart boy. Johnny is very lucky to get your blessings in his life. Your kindness and sympathy for others are very rare in any person and you possess them a lot. Then he looked at Johnny and said – come with me.

Head Master went out of the room and Balai Babu remained seated in the room. Sometimes later Head Master and Johnny came back into the room where Balai Babu was waiting. Balai Babu looked at the Head Master with curiosity and asked – how did it go?

Head Master looked at Balai Babu and said – sir, it went well in every subject in which I tested him except Math. He could not do any Algebra, in fact, Johnny never heard about Algebra. He is very ready for 8th grade but I am afraid that he would not be able to perform up to the standard unless he gets some extra help. I am telling him to go for grade 7 but he is insisting for grade 8. Honestly, I believe, if he studies hard and works extra hour for the Algebra he should be able to reach up to the standards of the class. So, I have decided to take him in 8th grade. Since then Johnny started the school in 8th grade and Head Master and his school teachers started to coach him on a daily basis and Johnny also started to show his merit and talent more and more.

With Balai Babu's kind blessings the candle of his life started to lighten little by little and Johnny's diligence and perseverance started to reward him in scholastic arena and in the final school leaving examination he created a rare example of the school when he stood third in the State and first in the district. His name came in newspaper, overnight Johnny became a star in the town, an ideal student in the school and a cause of proud complacence of the Head Master and Balai Babu. Even in the mist of all successes Johnny was very polite and humble and he took the blessings of all the teachers and Head Master by touching their feet and expressed his gratitude to all of them, he devoted his success to Balai Babu and his wife, Sheila. He told Balai Babu – Bapuji and Mataji, your blessings and kindness brought me to this point, the day I came in your family, I always regarded you and Mataji as my parents, my parents who gave me birth, they are birth parents but the real parents are you and Mataji. He bowed and touched their feet with due deference, his eyes were glittering with water and then said – Bapuji and Mataji, I want to get a shelter in your feet for all my life, please make sure that I always get your love and affection.

Balai Babu and his wife Sheila embraced him and said – Johnny, you will always be in our heart and you will always be our child, you will always receive our love and affection. Then said – now think, what you want to study in college, have you decided what you want to study?

Johnny said – Bapuji, I want to study medicine and become a doctor. Since my childhood when my mother passed away without any treatment in the hospital, at that time I decided to become a doctor and promised nobody will die without any treatment in the hospital where I shall work. I shall join the Medical College.

Hearing his desire to become a doctor Sheila said – very well. Then looked at her husband and said – please arrange his admission into Medical College. After that Johnny started his Medical College but never leave the house, he would still bring flowers for his Mataji so that she can pray to her house hold Gods Radha and Krishna. Sheila insisted many times not to do anymore but Johnny always refused to obey her and said – Mataji, I am doing it for my God, Bapuji and you, it gives me satisfaction that I am praying to my God and Goddess, please do not ask me to stop it, I want to worship my God as long as I live. Eventually this conversation had stopped and Sheila and Balai Babu started to feel that Johnny is their child and decided to give him any assistance to pursue his career in medical field. Both of them were very happy to see the wisdom in Johnny's heart.

Time flows like a river, never stops, and things change in every moment, eventually Johnny received his Medical Degree, he became the topper of the class, stood first in the state. Soon, he will join a hospital for his first job as a Doctor. The relation between Balai Babu's family and Johnny changed a long time ago, Johnny became a member of the family. He always discussed his ideas or decisions with Sheila and Balai Babu, or why should not he do it, they are his parents. Sheila and Balai Babu thought that if Johnny would go to England for his FRCS Degree, then he will be a well-trained and qualified doctor for this community and the community would receive his services and so many poor people would benefit by his expertise, this was the final decision by Johnny and his adopted parents.

Few weeks later Balai Babu gave a plane ticket for London to Johnny and said – here is your plane ticket for London, and some money for your expenses until you get your scholarship from your college. Although I do not have to mention to you, yet I am mentioning that stay focused and achieve your dreams, please try to write a letter to us once in every three months and thus we should be able to know how our Johnny Is doing in London. Your flight is tomorrow at 8 am in the morning. Ask your Mataji whatever you wish to eat before you leave for London. Balai Babu's voice became heavy, eyes were watery and heart was compassionate with the thought that they are going to separate from this boy in a few hours. Johnny was overwhelmed with Sheila and Balai Babu's love and affection and said – I shall put all my energy and devotion to study and with your blessings I shall come back as a FRCS Cardiologist that is what he wanted, to become a good Cardiologist. Next morning Head Master, Sheila and Balai Babu saw that the plane flew in the sky with their Johnny, gradually the plane vanished in the sky and their little Johnny entered into a new phase of life to become a Cardiologist.

Time flies before they realize, exactly similar way fifteen years passed by since Johnny left. In the beginning Sheila used to receive Johnny's letter very regularly until their son Nilay took over the business and sent away Sheila and Balai Babu into a small old broken house, water leaks from the roof, windows were broken, in other words it was a dilapidated house, lack of sun and fresh air made Balai Babu a heart patient but even after repeated requests Balai Babu and Sheila were never taken to any doctor for examinations or treatments, Sheila and Balai Babu basically were living a life of destitute, their son and daughter-in-law never gave them Johnny's letters and subsequently all the communications between Johnny and Balai Babu were severed, Johnny lost his adopted parents' touch, he felt, he became an orphan again for the second time. Johnny repented very much thinking that why he did not come to Balai Babu before, then this kind man would not have gone through so much misery and humiliation. Johnny could never thought that a kind man like Balai Babu and Mataji would ever raise a picaresque and Svengali like his son.

Two very kind persons' blessing hands were on top of Johnny's head. Johnny would never become a Cardiologist without the help of these two persons. So, he was always very grateful to both of them. So, after finding that Balai Babu and Mataji were in dire situation, he thought to find about the Head Sir and that was the reason he wanted to find out Head Sir and his wife's family situation. Then he decided to go to Head Sir's house, to find out about Head Sir and his wife whom he used call auntie. Johnny went to Head Sir's house and found that Head Sir has retired and sold his house and moved to a village. The new owner of the house said – that Anath Babu has moved to a small village and has bought a small house with some land. He is spending his retired days over there. He also mentioned the name of the village. Johnny found out the village where his Head Sir was living with his wife. Finally Johnny went to his

Head Sir's home in the village. One day in the morning Johnny reached Head Sir's home and he found that one old man is sitting on a chair and he was teaching a few children who were sitting on a rug in front him, Johnny went straight to him and touched his feet to express respect and then looked at Head Sir and said – sir, can you recognize me?

Head Sir being little perplexed with the question, looked at the person and said – son, I really do not know who you are, I understand you must be one my students but honestly I do not recognize you. Please tell me your name, he was apologetic to the person who asked him the question.

Then Johnny looked at Head Sir and said – I knew, you would not recognize me, since it has been a long time after I left for England. Sir, I am your student Johnny Jacob. Sir, I hope, now you recognize and remember me.

Suddenly Head Sir recognized him and embraced him and said – my favorite student Johnny, you have changed so much, and how would I think that you are our Johnny. Then he called his wife and said – look, who has come to see us, it is our Johnny, remember, you were talking about him the other day. Your favorite nephew is here. Head Sir's wife, Neela came running and saw Johnny standing there, and instantly said – son, you are Johnny, aren't you? She embraced Johnny and asked – Johnny, you look so different, how are you, son? Neela remembered, Johnny was a very sweet little boy, bright and polite and always smiling, no matter what, how can she forget a child like that. Neela remembered that every Sunday Johnny used to come to Head Sir's house for studying. This little shy boy would stay all day, sometimes would help her in household chores and Johnny used to call her Kakima (auntie), she felt her motherly affection for this boy and embraced him again and said – you sit with your Sir and I am going to bring your favorite snack of Samosa and tea. Johnny noticed that when Neela was walking, she looked very frail and was limping a bit, Johnny thought this auntie was so pretty and strong and now burden of age made her this fragile, aging is nothing but a curse in human life. Although peoples always say – old is gold but in reality it is a Pandora's box which contains all kinds of worms physical and mental maladies, olden years often become a painful and miserable experience of life time, Johnny thought, Head Sir, auntie Neela, Bapuji and Mataji are all victims of this minacious deluge of sufferance and pain for olden days. Bapuji and Mataji are perfect example of this heinous crime which are often committed by nearest and dearest ones who often disguise in the name of offspring, one's own children. It was about midday, Johnny wanted to leave but Neela auntie asked him to have lunch with them. Johnny could not refuse but was happy to see that his auntie was treating him like the old days.

During the lunch Johnny remembered that exactly same way Neela auntie used to give him food, only difference, that time all of them used to sit on the floor and now they were sitting on a dining table, Head Sir, Johnny and auntie were sitting face to face, Johnny asked – Sir, do you know how Bapuji and Mataji are living since their son took over the business?

Head Sir replied – yes Johnny, I know everything, his son and daughter-in-law never treated them well, finally shifted them into a broken down home, since then they are living in a very bad condition. I asked Balai Babu and Sheila to move in with us and stay with us but Balai Babu and his wife always refused our proposal very politely, then we moved in this village, since then I went to his house once only and at that time he thanked me a lot and said – Masterji, life is very strange, rich or poor, nobody knows what is coming next in anybody's life. I never thought that my own flesh and blood would betray me so much, just for the money. He was very sad and he repented and blamed themselves for raising a rogue son who would not care for his own parents. But whenever I met him, he always mentioned you and was concerned how you were doing, he also mentioned that in the beginning Johnny was writing a letter every three months but that letter has stopped long time ago, I hope him doing well.

Listening to Head Sir, Johnny said – now I understand why I did not receive any letter from Babuji, probably his son and daughter-in-law have never given my letters to them. I always wrote them every three months until I came back here. Now I understand very well why I never received a letter from Babuji and Mataji. Mataji and Bapuji became victims of family torture and deception. Johnny wanted to know how Debi the daughter of Head Sir was doing, he remembered that Debi and Johnny used to play sometimes when he was going to Head Sir's house. Auntie Neela said – Johnny, she is a doctor now and works in a hospital in the city. She comes home every few months and stays couple of days and then leaves. She did not marry and she always avoids the question "are you planning to marry someday? Her simple answer – not now, was always daunting to the parents, but parents did not want to force anything on her free will, she was busy with her work and spent most of the time in the city. After the lunch, Johnny bowed to do 'Namaskar" and said – Sir, I have to go now, I shall try to come back next week with Bapuji and Mataji here to meet you both. He sat on the car and asked the driver to leave for the hotel where he was staying. All his childhood reminiscences started to come in his mind, how this Head Sir and his wife used to shower their love, caring and affection on him, he would always remember their kindness.

Next day Johnny went to Bapuji's house. Bapuji and Mataji were sitting on the front of the house. Bapuji and Mataji were very happy when they saw Johnny in their house. They asked Johnny to sit on the bench where they both were sitting and then asked – Johnny, did you see Masterji?

Johnny replied – yes, Bapuji, I went to Head Sir's home yesterday and spent a few hours with them. He described how happy he was to meet them, Head Sir has taken a task to teach the poor children of the village and eventually to open a school for them. He also mentioned that Head Sir and auntie would very much love to see you and Mataji. So, if you give me permission then we can go to Head Sir's house next Sunday. Balai Babu listened to Johnny and said – Johnny, what is the use of going to him? He has asked me many times to move in with him and his wife but that we could not do anymore, we did not want any pity or mercy or favor from anyone, let us face our last days the way it may come to us. However, after some conversations Johnny was able to convince Bapuji and Mataji to go to Head Sir's home in next week on Sunday.

Johnny came to his hotel with Bapuji and Mataji. He brought them to his room and asked them to sit on the couch. His room was big and beautiful, had couches, and mirrors on the wall. Balai Babu remembered when he used to go for tour many years ago, used to stay in rooms like this. Both of them were sitting, Johnny ordered some cold drinks, then he turned to Bapuji and Mataji and hold their hands and pulled them towards a desk and opened his suitcase and took out a picture frame which contained an old picture of Johnny's Bapuji and Mataji, he showed the picture which he took from Mataji when he went to England and said – Mataji, remember, I took this photo from you because I wanted to have you both with me when I was in London, since then I always start my days by worshiping my God of my life, you and Mataji, now I pray to both of you that you come and stay with me so that I get a chance to pray to my living god every day of my life, please do not decline to approve my prayer and let me take care of my parents like you and Mataji, all I want is to get a chance to serve my own god who has made me whatever I am today, by saying he folded his hands and kneeled down to Bapuji and Mataji and said – please allow me to put you on the altar of my heart and worship you all my life.

After hearing Johnny Bapuji and Mataji both embraced Johnny and said – son Johnny, from now on we shall stay together with you until our mundane lives come to an end.

Johnny rented the President's suite of the hotel which had three bed rooms so that he could stay with his Bapuji and

Mataji. He was extremely happy to realize that his Bapuji and Mataji have agreed to live with him for the rest of their lives.

Next few days Babuji and Mataji were spending their times in the hotel while Johnny took permission to spend time outside for his future plans. He called all his architects to make plans for his hospital, school and a house where Mataji and Bapuji would live with Johnny. He found the land next to Head Sir and already has booked the land for purchase. He went in details with the architects how he wanted the hospital building, school building and his own residence. He explained to the architects that he wanted the building to be located in three corners of the land and the remaining fourth corner would be a place for his Bapuji and Mataji's Radha Krishna's Temple with a flower garden. This garden would become the primary source of flowers to pray to God and he himself would pick up the flowers as he did when he was a child and was living with Mataji and Bapuji. He wanted to become the real Johnny to them even though he was a famous Cardiologist to other peoples of the town. He wanted Bapuji and Mataji to feel that they were living with their son Johnny and he would keep no stones unturned to make them very happy and normal while they were living with him. He wanted a family which he lost many years ago when he lost his father in riots and mother in hospital untreated, this nightmare always came in his mind and sometimes even in dreams, he did not want to repeat this with his Bapuji and Mataji. Life without family, love and affection is meaningless to anyone and Johnny learnt it hard way, he did not want to go through the same hell again.

Johnny went to Head Sir's house with Bapuji and Mataji. He took the plans of the land with him. Once they reached Head Sir's home they found that Sir's daughter Debi also came home to meet Johnny. In their childhood they were playing together, picking flowers for the praying of Radha Krishna of Mataji's temple. Childhood reminiscence came into his mind, Debi was very thin, now she looked perfect with her long shinny hairs, and she looked very attractive with the same mischievous smile. Debi looked at Johnny and thought, my god, Johnny turned out to be very handsome guy, who would think that this Johnny was the same Johnny who looked little nervous and pale in those days. All of them sat on the dining table and Debi came back with some snacks and put them on the table and said – please start eating first, then we shall start talking. She then turned to Balai Babu and said – uncle, you like samosa very much, mom and I made them for you, please take them. She turned to Sheila and said – auntie, I know you like Papri Chat and I have brought it from the city for you, please take them. Then she turned to Johnny and said – sorry, I could not make anything special for you because you are a Sahib now, I do not know what you like but I think you still like Pakora, so I have some Pakora for you, now start eating them. They started to eat and speak about the old days, everyone was smiling and happy to ruminate the old days.

In middle of this gossip Johnny opened the plans for the land started to show his plan for the hospital, school, house, temple and the garden nearby the temple. Johnny's Architect made all these plans to make sure that they all could be with one another and he could serve the local peoples for their medical needs,

Head Sir could have a school for the destitute children of the village. In this meeting they have also decided the name of the school and the name of the Hospital.

After explaining the plans Johnny said – to Head Sir and Bapuji, I have received so much love and blessings from both of you, both of you believed in me, today I beg your permission to name the School as "Anath Bandhu Vidya Niketan" and the Hospital as "Balaram Sheila Arogya Niketan". It may take about one year to finish the construction of this project. Then she turned to Debi and said – Debi, I need your help to run this hospital, would you help me? All of us will live close by and serve the needy peoples of these villages, and nobody would die for the lack of treatment or medicine, with your help and expertise we shall make this a dream hospital where patients will recover, not succumb to any malady. This way children would get their education and become good productive citizens of the country, they would give back to the society a better place where prosperity and happiness would prevail.

After hearing Johnny's proposal Debi said – it would be a privilege for me to join such a noble mission. She also thanked Johnny for giving her a chance to serve the peoples of the villages. She also added Johnny, you are a great human being who thought about the underprivileged lives of a very poor rural area.

Johnny smiled and replied to Debi – Debi it is my privilege to have you in our project. Thank you very much for joining our mission.

Both families were overwhelmed to see Johnny's compassion for giving back to the society where he came from and his enormous gratitude for the peoples who have helped to build his career was praiseworthy.

In the middle of this Balai Babu started smiling and saying to Head Sir – Masterji, I have a request to you, with your permission, I want to tell you, Johnny is our son and he is a handsome charming young man, your daughter is a very beautiful and smart young lady, I want to beg your daughter's hand to unite with my son Johnny's hands, I think they will be a perfect match for each other, I want Debi to become our daughter-in-law, we are inviting her to take a place in our family.

Then he looked at Johnny and Debi and said – now I rest my case to you both, please give your verdict, yes or no. He pulled Debi in his arms and said – come and join my family, and also asked Johnny to come to his arms and asked Masterji and Neela to approve this union of the families. Johnny and Debi became very shy and smiling and expressed their approval of the relation and both of them bowed down and touched the feet of their parents and asked for their blessings.

This thing happened so quickly that Masterji and his wife bewildered with a vacant look in their eyes towards Balai Babu and said – we are extremely pleased to see that my daughter is going to your family as Johnny's wife, my only request to Johnny, please make our Debi a very happy married woman and today we have found a son whom we never had in our family, Johnny, welcome to our family, they both hugged Debi and Johnny and blessed them for their marriage.

Being inundated with blessings, Johnny became very passionate and said – Bapuji, Mataji, Head Sir and Auntie, today is the most happiest day of my life, today I received a partner of my life, I promise, I shall make every effort to make Debi a happily married wife, I lost my family many years ago, never thought that I shall get my family back again, today I got my life back, today I promise, I shall try to become a good son, a good son-in-law and above all a good husband for Debi, please bless me so that I can keep my promise, this became an auspicious day to all of them because all of them became bonded together as a family, especially Johnny's family.

LETTER TO OUR GRAND CHILDREN

—

The grandchildren are the most precious and invaluable members of any family's life. We became very lucky when our first grandchild was born in our two families namely Chakrabarti and Rotundo families in a cold morning of February of 2016. Both families rushed to the hospital to greet the new baby in both families. When my wife and I reached the hospital, we found that Rotundo family was already waiting in the waiting room of the hospital. When both families saw each other, they congratulated each other for becoming the new grandparents. For the first time when we have seen you, your eyes were closed, you looked divine, all of us fall in love with you and felt very blessed to have you in our family. You were lying down in your mom's lap, your eyes were closed, you looked like an angel, I picked you up from your mom's lap and I felt that I was holding a child who was a gift from God. You looked so pretty and calm in my arms that your Mimi (grandmother) said to me – you look like a very proud grandfather. Your Rotundo family and our family both agreed with later that was one of the best mornings of our lives when we met you for the first time. We were looking at you but you had your eyes closed, probably you felt - you were most safe in the arms of your mom. Few days later you came to your home with your mom and an enjoyable celebration took place to welcome you in your home for the first time. Both grandparents' families attended this family only celebration, your uncle Dan, your parents and we were so happy to see you in your home for the first time. The second wave of happiness inundated our families when our second grandchild, a girl put her feet for the first time in the world and our families were flooded with happiness to greet this angel in this world. Now, these two families were extremely thankful to God to have a boy and a girl in the family. Their parents named them according to their wish but all four of us, grandparents named them according to our wish, but these were their nick names and these names were only for us to call them, not for everyone else.

When you both became seven months old, we celebrated your first rice ceremony when your uncle Dan offered you first solid food which is rice pudding cooked by your Mimi, your father became the conductor of the celebration, but after eating the first rice you went to sleep. Your guests came to meet you but you went to deep sleep. Some of your guest had to leave without meeting you. This party of rice ceremony was a grand success all the guests were happy to eat, drink and be merry with food and drinks. You stepped into a new phase of your life and we were very happy to enjoy becoming a part of this grand party. Since then our lives are circling around you two only.

Little by little you started to grow up. All of us remember when you sat for the first time, when you started to crawl for the first time, both of you acted similar, only difference I remember is that Dom, you were crawling much faster than your sister Vera and amazingly when both of you took the first step on your first birth day, that lead us to celebrate big on both times, and why not, that was also your birthday celebration also, as you started your journey towards growing up, we also became fellow passengers in this journey of yours'. As time started to pass by, you two started to learn new life skills almost on a daily basis, two of you would be naughty to one another, brother was taking away sister's toy and runaway, sister would catch you up and take her toy forcibly from brother, but when sister would snatch any toy from you (brother), then you would come running to your Mimi and complain – Mimi, she took my toy, please tell her to give it back to me. By the time you have finished your complaint your sister ran away from you. At that time Mimi would catch your sister and made her return your toy. When we were taking you guys to any playground, Dom would start running fast and often say – Babi, I am superfast, you cannot catch me. Dom would continue to run and it would be real tough for me to catch him for an old man like me. In comparison to Dom, Vera was lot easier, she would run but lot slower than Dom. You would stay for two three hours in the park, your Mimi and I would be very tired to take even one step but you two would still like to stay in the park. Vera and you often leap on your toes, we hardly have seen you walk in the house, leaping on toes were your habits. It looked very funny and your Mimi and I enjoyed every bit of it. Occasionally two of you would be fighting with one another and then Mimi had to stop your fight, most of the times it would be with toys, once in a while it would be with food. For Dom, food was not that important but Vera, you loved to eat, most of the times you would be the invader who would snatch food from your brother, and this was brother and sister game you were playing with one another all the times. However, on many instances, Dom, you have acted as a big brother, one example one day you were playing in our deck, you dropped your favorite toy and you started crying and guess who got that toy soon, none other than your brother tom. Vera, during those days you used to call Dom as brother, after receiving the toy from Dom, you said – brother, thank you. And your brother hugged you and said – Vera, don't cry, I shall bring your toy again if you drop it again. We, your grandparents, were overwhelmed by watching the love, care and affection between brother and sister.

Every day, I used to get up early in the morning and sit on my recliner in the bed room and open my computer and check all my mails and watch the news on television, this was my habit, and have a cup of tea. You two would be sleeping in a different room with your grandma Mimi. After you get up from your bed two of you always rushed to my bed room, show the side of the chair and tell – Babi, I want to sit here. Before I could realize two of you jump on my chair and squeeze yourselves in my chair on my left and right side making me a sandwich and start playing with the key board of the computer, and compel me to stop whatever I was doing, two of you would take over my computer and start playing. Whenever you guys slept over, I used to long for this moment of morning, those were the most enjoyable moments of my life.

Your mother's rule – you cannot watch cartoons before 8 am in the morning, but every morning two of you would insist to watch it anyway. Children are the best negotiators in the world, their most useful argument of negotiation is crying, you were doing the same thing, you cried and signed the deal, your cartoon is on the TV immediately. One day Dom, you asked me – Babi, guess what?

I replied – what?

You started laughing and leaping and said – Chicken butt. Vera heard this joke and she came running to me and said – Babi, guess what?

Same way I replied – what?

She started laughing and said – chicken "bupp". At that time she could not pronounce "t". So "chicken butt" became "chicken bupp" for her. At that time all of us started to laugh. Two of you have made fun of me by using this "chicken butt/bupp" phrase for next few weeks. Two of you were so mischievous that you were inventing a new one on a daily basis and were playing with us very joyfully. Normally when you two were in our house we were giving you living room and foyer for your activities and I used work in the bed room. One of your favorite game was to put all the pillows on the floor and make a line and ask me walk over those, I would pretend that I could not walk, then both of you hold my both hands and make me walk over the pillow and tell – Babi, this is how you walk, next time you have to walk by yourself. Okay Babi. And smilingly I used to say – okay Dommy dada and Vera didi. Next day you would repeat this pillow line and I would miss that walk and both of would be frustrated and tell – Babi, you forgot not that way and show me again, at point your Mimi would come to rescue and ask me to do something and save from the situation. Your creativity of doing naughty stuff was amazing and both of us always enjoyed these small depravities which two of you were doing all the times. I am sure when you grow up and read about these mischiefs which two of you have done as a child must enjoy reading about this naughty stuff. Now I am going to mention one other thing which you brother and sister have done once. I was sitting on my recliner in the bed room and working in computer at that time two of you came and wanted to sit with me in your usual way, I said – not now, I have to finish it soon, we will sit later on, please give a little time but you guys were insisting, so, I said – okay come and sit quietly with me and let me finish it, at that time your Mimi came to ask me something, suddenly two of you got up from the chair and ran to the door and lock the room from outside, and started saying – Babi, you are locked in the room, you cannot come and catch us. By the time we opened the door and got up to you we found that two of you have opened the pantry and taken two boxes of chips and started to eat them, when your Mimi wanted to catch you guys, you started to drop chips all over the living room, finally your Mimi caught you guys and gave chips in separate bowls to you for eating. When you grow up and read about it, I hope, you would remember how naughty you two guys were. You were little naughty, were expert in doing mischiefs, it was okay, that was your age to do it, we were never angry with anyone of you, we rather enjoyed your creativity of depravity, we always prayed to god for your wellbeing. We have always loved you to our heart's content.

Now I shall come to a different point, a point which describes the ancestry of you two brother and sister. You have been born in a family where your both parents come of a very rich and special civilization of the world. By this age you probably have come to know that your father's family came from Italy and your mother's family migrated to USA from India. Since many centuries ago Italy was the pedestal of arts, literature, performing arts, music and culture of the world, what Italy did, whole Europe wanted to follow and enrich themselves with the civilization of Italy. Roman Empire was the most famous empire which started in 27 BC and ended in 753 BC. The Roman Empire thrived to a new cultural height in the 9th century and was very dominantly reigning in culture and arts etc. Your father's family is the part of that glorious cultural history of Italy. Your mother's family is embedded in the ancient Indian Cultural Ocean of philosophy. When your father's and mother's family joined together, the profound teachings of science of Western World and the wisdom of Indian culture and philosophy mingled together to create a Unique mix of two worlds in your lives, East and West, always be proud of your rich heritage and please try to carry them for your children, this way it will continue for many generations to come.

Remember, your parents are your best friends and well-wishers, they will always be there for both of you no matter what, always be truthful and sincere to them even if you make a mistake. Lying once will lead to many lies and eventually you will be caught and you will be in more trouble, on the other hand if you tell the truth they will understand and advise you not to make the same mistake again. During the period of your growing up you will go to School and then to College hopefully to educate yourselves. Education is the manifestation of perfection already in human. Education gives you knowledge and knowledge is power When you go to School and College, you nurture and shine your inner qualities which will guide you to a better path of life, this education will eventually put you to your highest potential altar of life. Education gives you knowledge and knowledge is power. This power of knowledge will always show you the right path in your life. So, make sure that you work hard to achieve this education in yourselves. This education will definitely lead you to become a decent human being who would care for the wellbeing of others and for the society as well. Education has also another unique quality, whoever has it, nobody can take away by force, nobody can steal or rob it from anyone, once someone possesses it, it is for him forever, it is the best weapon to face any difficult situation of life, so it is not optional rather it is mandatory that you educate yourselves to the highest level of scholastic degree possible. Every human being must possess this for the benefit of his or her life. There is a saying "A king is only revered by the subjects of his Kingdom but an Educated Scholar is revered by everybody in the world." So, Education is a must for every human being including you two. Once you achieve your education, automatically you will enrich yourself with a correct moral character. Character can be good; it can also be bad. Character can be defined as the combination of qualities like truth, honesty, sincerity, selflessness, do good to other human beings etc., anyone who possesses all these qualities is a person of "good character", and anyone who is devoid of any of these qualities is usually a person of a "not good character". As a decent human being, everyone should be a person of good character. Always respect women, they are equally smart like men, in some cases they are smarter, give them their due respect, then you will enjoy the deep love and affection of a mother, a sister and a wife, and your life will be very easy and enjoyable. Also remember – respect begets respect, it is a two-way process. Human beings live in a social structure, every society has its norms and socially accepted behavior, as a decent human beings all of us should follow those contemporary and prevalent accepted behaviors, only then a human being can be a person who can enrich his society, and thus makes the community a better place to live and flourish as a society.

In your life you will come across situations which will make you very upset or angry, this is part of human life, never let this situation control you, rather you control the situation, control your anger and walk away from it and forget it, and try to regain your emotional composure soon. If you walk away, it does not make you small or coward, it rather shows that you are a smart person who controls the odd situation. During the course of our living we will face many obstacles in lives, we will get many successes in our lives, do not let these events control you rather try to take both under your control and try to be graceful and accept them as a routine part of any human life. If you ever feel that you have done anything wrong to anyone, the moment you realize, beg forgiveness immediately from the person whom you did wrong, it will not make you small, it will rather implicate the strength and courage of your character, similarly if anyone does anything wrong to you, first you let him know that you did not like it and then try to forgive him whether he begs for it or not, remember - forgiveness is divine and it shows the strength of character of a person. Real education teaches us to become humble and being humble is not weakness, it rather makes a person just and dignified.

In the journey of your life, you will always see some of your fellow human beings are not in a good position, financially or any other way, please try to alleviate their situation, helping others is a quality which all of us should possess. In this respect I shall depict what my father told me when I was a teen ager and it was – "son, always try to share your good luck with those who do not have it, this way you will be blessed by the God, and giving never reduces your good luck, also always be satisfied whatever situation you are in, then you will never be poor, only the unsatisfied person is the poor." I made this advice of my dad as the "Mantra" of my life and tried to follow them all my life till now. We are blessed with life, life is beautiful and enjoy every moment of it, every day is beautiful, you may not get tomorrow as beautiful as today, so be happy with today and accept whatever comes tomorrow.

I wish, I could be a part of your growing up as teen agers but considering my age, I believe, probably I shall not be blessed with that opportunity but my eyes and blessings for your wellbeing will always remain on you until you become a good human being for your parents, for your families and for the society as a whole.

As grandparents, it is our dream that our grandchildren will someday become a decent and contributing member of the community, and we dream that someday you will make us proud to feel that we are part of you and we will be living in you as a family. Although our mundane lives may not the here but our souls will always be here with both of you whenever you need our advice or blessings, we will be there and you will feel it in your hearts, two of you always be our grandchildren and we shall always be your grandparents.

N.B. Names are imaginary

MODI'S HISTORIC VISIT

⁓

Peoples lined up for half a mile, waited for hours to witness the historic visit of Prime Minister, Narendra Damodardas Modi in Madison Square Garden of Manhattan. Security was very tight, all the roads surrounding the Madison Square Garden were blocked for regular traffic, and all you could see is hundreds of police officers including the canine units. More than four hundred organizations including Cultural Association of Bengal took part to create this new history of relationship between USA and India where NRIs are acting as prime catalyst. Madison Square Garden area was flooded by non-resident Indian population. Men, women and children all were anxiously waiting in line to enter the Madison Square Garden. They were here to witness the historic moment from all over the United States; NRIs from East, West, North and South all mingled here in this huge assemblage of crowd in Madison Square Garden. Finally waiting came to an end. At about 10:45 am the organizers announced that the program will start soon.

The program started with the national anthems of both countries of India and USA. The entertainment started with a

Rajasthani folk dance performed by Gujrati performers. Mrs. Kavita Krishnamurthy's song

"..love India" mesmerized the audience. After this the dignitaries started to assemble on the stage. Senators and Congressmen of tri-state area namely Sen. Chuck Schumer, Sen. Cory Booker, Cong. Nita Lowey and few others came on the stage to greet Prime Minister Mr. Narendra Modi. In the meantime the assemblage started to chant "Modi, Modi" at the top of their voice. At last waiting was over, Mr. Modi entered the Garden being surrounded by NYC Police and his personal Security Guards. Everybody stood up and greeted him with clapping of hands for minutes together, felt like welcoming is not going to end. One could feel the whole crowd was electrified by the spirit of love for the motherland, India.

Mr. Modi saluted the crowd by folding his hands and bringing them close to his forehead. Then he started by saying " Bhaiyo aur Beheniyo", hearing him peoples started to clap so loudly that Mr. Modi had to pause for a few minutes then he said " you have migrated to America and by doing this you have increased the prestige of India by your hard work, intelligence and education, we are proud of you all." In his speech he mentioned " when world's largest and oldest democracy work together, only good things can happen to the world, the world can only go forward for brighter days, sixty five percent of Indian population is thirty five years old or younger, with this magnitude of strength youth India can lift any burden for the betterment of human kind." He also said "the government is there to serve the public not to become the master, even a sweeper can take part to take the country forward by doing his job, I want to cleanse the environment, mother Ganges needs to be pollution free, I need your help to make mother Ganges pollution free so that our parents can bathe in the holy river, will you help us, he asked the crowd in the Garden." The crowd spontaneously replied "yes, yes and yes". By virtue of Bikash policy India would be a big work force and Indians will spread all over the globe with their expertise. He promised lifelong visa for PIO card holders. He also promised that PIO/OCI card holders will get same benefit, he admitted it is difficult to obtain visa from Consulate, consequently he also promised that US Citizens will get visa on arrival at the port of entry. He promised "you have given me a chance to serve you, this sevak will leave no stones unturned to serve you and your purpose, and in the end he promised with your help and our tireless hard work I shall deliver you the Hindustan of your dream. He ended his speech by saying "Bharat Mata Ki Jay".

MY CIVIC DUTY

—

In the summer of 2003, I received a letter from the Southern District of New York, US District Court, Department of Jury Selection. They sent me a questionnaire to answer and asking me to return it to them within a specified time. At first I did not pay attention to it because over the years I have received these many times. All I had to do is to call them and mention that I am a health professional and my services as potential Juror was always excused. With the same hope I called the Jury Manager of Southern District one day and the voice on the other side wanted to know – who is calling.

I mentioned my name in her query and said – madam, I am a pharmacist, please excuse me from this Jury duty. I am self-employed and it will be impossible for me to close the pharmacy to attend the Jury duty. So, I requested her again to excuse me.

She replied – yes, you are right, we have excused you before because of your profession. But now the law has been changed and every profession has been included. So, it does not matter anymore whether someone is in medical profession or any emergency profession. Everybody has to render this service if selected. If you do not comply with it, you can go to jail according to the present law. So, my advice to you – fill out the questionnaire and return it within the specified time. Otherwise you could be in legal trouble. She explained the whole situation very nicely and politely.

After the conversation I realized – I am on the hook for it. This time there is no escape in sight. Now I have to arrange for a substitute employee to work for me when I shall be out for Jury duty. In those days it was not easy to find a pharmacist for work. Demand was very high and supply was very low, it was a very tough situation for me. So, I stopped thinking about it. I put my mind in filling the questionnaire. I have to return it within next seven days.

Eventually I mailed the information to the Jury Manager and started to concentrate to find a pharmacist who will work in my absence in the pharmacy. In this country nobody can open the door of a pharmacy for business without the presence of a licensed pharmacist. A Pharmacist is the soul of the pharmacy business. I decided to wait until I am called for the Jury duty.

A few days later I got a letter from the Jury Manager. She asked me to attend on a specific date and time in her office for becoming a prospective Juror. Her office was located in White Plains in Westchester County. It was not far from my home, may be 12 miles. It should not take me more than 25 minutes to go to her office. Since I did not have a GPS, I wrote down the direction for the place. I reached there about 10 minutes late because I had hard time finding a parking space. The young lady in the office told me – please sign this paper and give me your parking ticket, I shall put the stamp on the back of it then you don't have to pay for it.

I signed the paper and told her – I parked on the street. I do not have a parking ticket, so you don't have to stamp.

She looked at me and said – next time when you come here, park in any of the parking garages nearby, we will pay for your parking, you don't have to waste your time by trying to find a parking spot on the street. She smiled at me. Then said – please have a seat, if you want please take some tea or coffee, also donut is there you may take them as well. Please be patient, in next half hour Jury Manager will come and guide you for your today's activity. I thanked her and took a seat in a nearby chair. I decided not to drink any coffee.

I was looking around the room. It is a big room. It can accommodate about hundred fifty peoples. It has a small stage in one end and a small podium on the stage. Many peoples were there in the room. Some of them are talking to the next person, some are reading books, some are doing nothing but having a vacant look in the face, and I was sitting quietly in a corner, thinking about how I can avoid this duty. Suddenly I heard – is this your first time? This question came from a middle aged woman. I should say – she is a pretty woman. She smiled at me.

I looked at her and said – yes, this is my first time. I tried to keep it short. But she is a type of person who likes to mingle and talk to others. She said – previously I have been selected two times, I hope, this time they do not select me. I have things to do in this week, besides I am self-employed, if they select me, probably I have to keep my store closed. I have to put a notice saying – on vacation, do not know when will be back. I have to lie to my customers. Then she asked me – how about you? What you do for a living. Before I could answer her, I heard someone was saying here comes the Jury Manager. I could not reply to her.

A very young woman appeared on the podium. She looked very pretty in her dark navy blue suit. Her appearance perfectly matched with her personality, her face was bright with a pleasing smile. She took the microphone and started to say – good morning, ladies and gentlemen, thank you very much for coming here this morning. We appreciate that you have responded to our request to help our judicial system. As a citizen of this great country, we all have our duties and obligations to the country. As we all enjoy the rights and privileges as a citizen, it also our duty to serve the country when the country needs us. Army protects the country from outside enemies, same way you will be protecting our justice system from injustice by sitting on the Jury Bench. Some of you may think that you have to become a legal expert to sit on the Jury Bench, but it is not. I am going to explain to you how the judicial system works. If you are selected for the Jury duty, all you have to do is to hear the arguments of the lawyers attentively, and use your common sense to determine whether the defense attorney or prosecuting attorney is making any sense to you. Believe me, you will know when it makes sense and when it does not. You do not need special training for it, we are engaged in this Jury duty in our daily activities. If you notice every day we make our decisions depending on our judgements, exactly this is what you will be doing as a Juror. Then she smiled and said – don't be nervous, you have no reason to be nervous, believe me, you will be fine. Just use your common sense. Please fill in this form correctly and truthfully. She showed us a form in her hand and said – you will get this form in a few moments. Before I give you the form, I have to explain two more things. As a prospective Juror we will divide you all in a few groups, each group will consist of twenty persons. You will be interviewed by the Judge, defense attorney and prosecutor of the case, if they do not select you do not feel bad, it does not mean that you are bad or unfit person for becoming a Juror, it only means that you did not fit the criteria of the case. Judge and attorneys of both sides want to make sure that the person whom they select should be able to serve their purpose of the related case. If you are selected, you will have to come every day to hear the case until you give the verdict at the end of the trial. We understand – your time is very valuable, that is why after today's attendance, you will not be required to serve as Juror for next three years. We shall give you a certificate, please keep it for next three years, if you are called by mistake or by other courts, just let them know that you have attended today's session. Now if you have any question, I shall try to answer them. She explained the whole thing so well that nobody had any question. She announced – since you do not have any question, I am going to distribute this form, please fill it carefully and truthfully because the Judge and attorneys of both sides will ask you questions on the basis of the information which you will provide in this form. At the end she gave a big smile and said – thank you very much and we wish you all the best in your Jury duty. Then she left.

The form was not difficult. Basically it wanted to know have you ever been convicted of any crime, if there is a pending criminal case against you or if anyone of your family or you are a part of any civil litigation or if there was any judgement pending against you. The form did not pose any threat to me. I felt very intimidated thinking that I am going to determine someone's fate just by being on the Jury Bench. In my heart and mind I felt that it is a huge burden on my honesty, integrity truthfulness and judgement. I got very nervous just by thinking about the fact that I am going to decide someone's fate; when I have never met the person or heard about him, this situation made me very nervous and I started to pray that god gives me the strength to render my duties truthfully and honestly. I was deeply absorbed in my thoughts, I completely forgot that I was sitting in a room where everybody is talking, laughing, creating a hue and cry, seemed to me that these peoples did not understand the gravity and burden of sitting on Jury Bench. My stomach started grumbling, I felt that I should go to the bath room. I got up to go to the bath room.

When I came back, I found that our group has been called by a Judge. All of us got up and started to go towards his court room. One assistant from Jury Office was guiding us to the Judge's Court. Finally he took us to the court room and said – please go inside and be seated. Someone from the court will advise you what to do. The Judge's Court was a big room. There was a medium stage at the end of the room, a big desk and a chair are on the stage, clearly understandable they were for the Judge. In the back of the chair there was a national flag with the eagle. I noticed a computer screen on the desk. Below the stage I saw a shorthand machine and a chair. When I entered the room, I noticed there were four rows of bench for the audience who will watch the trial. After that the room has been divided in two equal portions. Each portion had a small podium with a small microphone, then big table with four chairs. I realized that these must be the table for the defense and prosecutorial attorneys. Room looked very neat and attractive. It was very unique to see the Judge seated in front of the flag. I already started to feel the presence of truth and justice in the environment of the room. My nervousness started to fade away, I started to feel confident that I would be able to carry my duty truthfully and honestly to provide justice to someone who sought it.

After a few minutes, the bailiff announced – all rise, honorable Judge Mr. Justice Render is here. Judge entered the room and took seat and said – please be seated. Then he opened his computer. He took the file which was on the table, looked for something in it and then put it down. At that time the bailiff whispered in his ears and then said – ladies and gentlemen of prospective Jury, The judge and attorneys of prosecution and defense will call you and ask you a few questions on the basis of information which you have provided in the forms and then the Judge will let you know if you are selected for this case. Then he said – this is a civil case where the plaintiff is Ms. Jane Doe and the defendants are Valeria Mall, Police Officer John Smith, and the city of Bargain, New York.

The bailiff called my name and I got up and went to the Judge. I sat on a chair designated for the Juror. In front of me were two attorneys, we sat in front of the Judge making a half circle. The Judge looked at my answer sheet and asked – Mr. Wood, what is your profession?

I am a pharmacist – I replied. Hearing my answer the Judge told – I see you are involved in a litigation, please tell me about it. Before I could explain, the defense attorney said – Judge, I do not want him, he is involved in a litigation. Judge looked at the defense attorney and said – let us hear him. Please tell me what happened. Judge looked at me.

I told – your honor, I own a drug store, a wrong medicine was dispensed by our pharmacist to a patient and she was hospitalized by the unwanted action of the medicine. So, the patient has sued the pharmacy for her mental and physical sufferings and mental pains. I have given the notice to our Insurance Company. It happened about three months ago, the insurance company has taken the prescription, since then I did not hear from them. Once I called and asked the Insurance Company about it, the Insurance Company told me that they will take care of it; I do not have to worry about it, after that I do not know anything about this case.

Judge asked me – how do you feel about this woman, do you think she did the right thing by suing the pharmacy?

Sir, the lady suffered for the wrongful action of the pharmacy, in my opinion she should have some kind of compensation for her pain and suffering, I think, she has taken the correct decision against the pharmacy – was my reply

The Judge said – she sued your pharmacy and you still think she is right, you are not angry with her.

Sir, no, I am not angry, the fact is she suffered. Does not matter whose pharmacy is this, pharmacy should be punished for its negligence – I replied to the Judge.

After hearing my reply, Judge looked at the defense attorney who objected and said – now what you think about him? But he did not wait for the defense attorney's opinion, he looked at me and said – even though someone has sued your pharmacy, do you think that you can be neutral and consider the importance of evidence of the case, can you be devoid of personal bias about the accused in this case, can you assure your decision about the case will be solely on the basis of evidence and evidence only? He looked straight into my eyes, seemed he is trying to read my mind.

I replied – sir, I promise, I shall consider only the evidence to reach my decision, nothing else is going to influence to reach my decision, only the evidence will. The Judge told the defense attorney that he should include me in the Jury panel. The defense attorney nodded his head to show that he agreed with the Judge. After speaking to all of us they have selected ten of us to sit on the Jury panel. Judge instructed us to come to his court at 2 pm. The court will be in session at that time. All of us took a leave from the Judge. I looked at the watch and decided to go for lunch.

After lunch, all of us went to the court of Justice Render. Bailiff asked us to follow him and he took us in a room. This room was big. In one corner there is a coffee machine. There is a big oval shaped table which has twenty chairs around the table. Bailiff asked us to sit on the designated chairs by each name. He also said – from now on until the verdict of the case is rendered, you must sit on your designated chair. You cannot change your seat, no matter what. In case you want to change your position of the seat, you have to take Judge's permission. He gave us some time to be seated in our respective spots. Then he said – this case is about a woman who went through this ordeal has lodged a complaint to the Judge for her pain and suffering, I am mentioning this because you will have an idea about this trial. How you will perform your duty, the Judge will explain everything when you go to his court. Now you can relax and chat among yourselves and know each other because you will be spending next few days with one another. Now please excuse me. The room is all yours. See you in the court room in next fifteen minutes. He left the room.

After the bailiff left, we started to talk among ourselves. Out of ten Jurors three were women, and seven were men. I was amazed to see that this Juror's education was level from high school diploma to master's in chemistry. One guy was a mechanical engineer. Two of them were working as clerks in government and private office, one was stock clerk in a department store, and other seven including myself were professionals from all walks of life. Education does not mean anything here, the Judge asked us to weigh the evidence with reasonable commonsense only. We had some chit chat among ourselves, one thing was clear from these gossips, all of us were very concerned to deliver justice, all of us were a bit nervous about the fact that should we be able to find the truth in this trial, and deliver the truth to the judge. Suddenly we heard the announcement that Judge is coming into his court. Everyone stood up and Judge told us – please be seated. He explained the case to us briefly, he explained what we could do or could not, should we have any question about any statement or any word, we could ask the Judge to explain the meaning of it to us. He also forbade us not to come in contact with defense or plaintiff's attorneys, no matter what. We were not allowed to ride the same elevator if they were in there, we were not allowed to say – even words like 'good morning or good night' etc. Any kind of contact with them was forbidden.

The trial started. The Judge stated – I am the law in this court, any legal explanation, I give, must be adhered to, you must not, I repeat, you must not ask any question to any witnesses or attorneys; should you have any question about anything you must ask me, in this court you are not permitted to speak to anyone other than me, remember this advice or you may face the contempt of court. He was very clear to us. We understood the gravity of his advice.

This was a trial where Ms. Jane Doe was seeking for justice for her false arrest by police, false allegation against her by Valeria Mall, for humiliation, assassination of character, pain and sufferings of her mind and body. The plaintiff's attorney approached the Jury bench, smiled at us and said – it is a very clear case of violation of civil rights of Ms. Jane Doe by the Police Officer Town Protector, Town of Bargain and Valeria Mall. Plaintiff's attorney was a very beautiful woman, her personality was very pleasing and her charming smile could win anyone's mind. She smiled at us and said - once all the evidences and testimonies of witnesses are presented to you, it will be very clear to you that this woman was persecuted for nothing and she deserves the Justice in this court and I am very confident that you will deliver justice to her. She made her point and went back to her seat. All of us paid full attention to her speech, some of us also took notes from what she said, for me it was very interesting, what she said and the way she said, made an impact on all of us.

Then the defense attorney approached the Jury panel and said – from the support of the evidences and testimonies of the witnesses I shall prove to you that the Police Officer John Smith, the Town of Bargain and the Valeria Mall acted very properly and Ms. Jane Doe's rights were never violated, that's all, ladies and gentlemen of the Jury. Once you hear all the testimonies, you will have no choice but to dismiss all the charges against my clients. He stopped his speech there and took his seat.

Defense's first witness was a security guard of Valeria Mall. In his testimony he explained that he saw a person with a baseball cap in his head, looked like the person who was barred from entering the Mall. He was standing in next to the car which he drove to come to the Mall. He said – I could not see his face clearly because of his cap. He was convinced that he was the barred person. So he called his supervisor and his supervisor called the police. Seeing the police car coming in, she sat in her car and started the engine. At that point the police officer confronted her from the passenger side of the car and pulled her out through the driver side window of the car. At the cross examination of plaintiff's attorney, he also confirmed that this person was screaming "saying, let me go, it hurts, you cannot pull me through the window". His supervisor said that it seemed to him that police officer used excessive force to take her out of the car. When plaintiff's attorney asked – how you would take her out of the car. He replied – I would take her out by the passenger side of the car. Next few witnesses gave their version of the episode but nobody corroborated with one another. On the final day of hearing Police Officer Smith was called and in his testimony he described that he pulled the woman out through the driver side of the door and then arrested her for unlawful trespassing and loitering. When he was interrogated by the plaintiff's attorney – he said I was very polite and gentle with the woman but she was not cooperating and was cursing me and the Mall for arresting her. I acted very properly and professionally with the woman. Then I took her to my custody and transferred her to the police station. After listening to the Police Officer's testimony the plaintiff's attorney sought the Judge's permission to show the arresting incident in a video clip. Someone from the crowd taped the whole video till the police officer made her sit in the patrol car and left for the police station. All of us on the Jury Bench watched the video and found out that the testimony given by the Police Officer Smith was full with contradictions and the facts were distorted by Police Officer Smith to safeguard his own wrong doings. It became obvious to us that he committed perjury on the witness stand. When the video showing was completed the plaintiff's attorney said – as I mentioned before that this innocent lady has been violated and she deserves to receive justice and compensation for her sufferance of pain and humiliation of her person. This video has shown all the wrong doings to her by the Police Officer Smith, the Valeria Mall and the City of Bargain. Please deliberate with your common sense on the basis of all the given evidences and come up with the guilty verdict making them responsible for their illegitimate action. She stopped her summation.

The defense attorney came to us and started his summation. He started – ladies and gentlemen of the Jury, it is a very clear cut case of mistaken identity, where everybody was confused about the identity of Ms. Jane Doe. The security guards thought that she was that guy who was barred from entering the mall. The policeman tried to do his best so that Ms. Jane Doe does not get hurt when she was arrested. Also we have found that Mr. Smith's statement and video of the incidence did not match, because it took place three years back and he possibly forgot the details of this incidence. In last year Mr. Smith received a commendation from the police department for his honesty, bravery and his selfless service for the local community. In making your decision, you must consider the goodness of Mr. Smith who has put his life on the line to protect the neighborhoods of this Bargain Town. And if you consider these good acts, you can only find him not responsible for Ms. Jane Doe's pain and suffering, instead she is the one who should be held responsible for Smith her arrest and sufferance and consequently please come back and give a not guilty verdict. That is all I want to reiterate to you all.

After his summation, the Judge looked at his watch and looked at the Jury Bench and said – ladies and gentlemen, now you have heard the summations narrated by the attorneys of plaintiff and defense. You have heard and seen all the evidences and testimonies, now please make your decision solely on the basis of testimonies and the evidences only. If you have any question about any evidence, any witness's testimony, any legal explanation for any point, please get back to me, do not engage forming any opinion on the basis of any hearsay or any imaginary arguments those may be fair to you, it is my instruction to all of you that you decide the case strictly on the basis of all the testimonies beyond the reasonable doubt. I hope, you have understood my instructions, if you did not understand any part, please let me know now, I shall explain to you again. Judge also suggested – should you find the defendants guilty of wrong doing to Ms. Jane Doe, you must reward her monetarily for her defamation of character, pain and suffering, also you can recommend punishment for the police officer. Also remember, reward money should not exceed the amount more than they are seeking for. Also I like to remind you that you do not have to deliberate about her legal bills, I shall decide that amount. I also want to remind you that you can render one decision at a time or both together if you want to do so. Thank you very much and resume your duty as Juror of this case.

We entered the Jury room. But before we could settle down the bailiff came into the room and announced that the court has been adjourned now, the court will resume at 10 am tomorrow. You are dismissed for now, you will resume your duties tomorrow. Please do not discuss the case with anyone, and that includes your spouse too. Thank you very much, see you tomorrow.

The next morning all of us assembled in the Jury Room. We started to discuss the evidences and witnesses' testimonies, we concluded that none of us believed the testimony which was given by the Police Officer Smith. We also came to a conclusion that plaintiff's witnesses were very truthful and we had no doubt in our minds that Ms. Jane Doe was humiliated and she suffered in the hands of police, the mall and Town of Bargain. So, all of us decided unimanuously to render a guilty verdict against the defendants. Now we have to deal with the second part of the decision, monetary reward for Ms. Jane Doe. We started to deliberate on this issue. I proposed – let us decide the fate of Police Officer. In my opinion, being a lawman he broke the law and lied in the court. Majority of the Jury did not accept my proposal, they wanted to show some leniency to the police officer. Someone came up with a proposal to fine him for $ one dollar and stop the raise for next 3 years. Someone else had the idea of fining him one hundred thousand dollars and stopping the raise for next ten years. However, none of these proposals made any cut in our deliberation. Finally, after numerous discussions we came to a conclusion that we must be just to the police officer, we should not treat him harshly, and rather we should show our impartiality towards him. At last we came to a consensus that we will impose a fine for forty thousand dollars and stop the yearly raise for four years. One part was done but the harder one is waiting for us, now we have to determine the amount of compensation for her pain and suffering. For that we have to consider her age, education, employment, salary and loss of salary etc. During the trial we came to know that Ms. Jane Doe had an associate degree, she was working for a bank for a moderate salary, after being arrested she lost that job, her friends looked down upon her, she was mentally oppressed by her acquaintances, she was ashamed and suffering from inferiority complex. Now we have to weigh her situation and try to compensate her losses accordingly. All of us started to think how we can deliver justice to Ms. Jane Doe. All of us felt the burden on our shoulders. It is very easy to think of delivering justice, but when it is your responsibility to deliver, the whole dynamic changes, my conscience started to prick me, I was afraid, what if I fail to discharge my duties as Juror, all these thoughts mad me real nervous. It was a big question for all of us how we determine the parameter of legitimate number, then put a dollar amount on it for her pains and sufferings. We did not have any magical stunt to do it but we had ten dedicated minds to accomplish it. Our spokesman of the Jury said – I have an idea, let us put the dollar amount in a piece of paper, whatever individually we feel is the right amount of compensation. His suggestion seemed to be reasonable at that moment. So, we put a dollar amount in small papers. Ten jurors, ten minds, ten pieces of small papers and we had ten different dollar amounts, seemed to be our magical solution for the puzzle. We had ten different dollar amounts. One of the jurors suggested that we discard the highest and the lowest amounts which were suggested, then take the average of the remaining numbers and make that number as the dollar amount of compensation. I thought, it was an interesting idea and I also remembered that I heard about it somewhere but I could not remember where I heard about it. Anyway, that is not important. After all discussions we took the average of all eight numbers except the highest and the lowest numbers and came to 523 thousand dollars and all of us agreed to round it up to 525 thousand dollars. Although some of us argued this amount is not enough for her humiliation, pain and suffering, others took the position that this amount is too small to compensate her loss, so we started to talk about the amount and finally came to a consensus that 525 thousand will be the amount for her loss. All of us were very happy that we could fulfill our responsibility as Juror and then our spokesman went to the bailiff and informed that we have finished the deliberation and the verdict is ready for the Judge.

At the request of the bailiff we entered the court room and took our seats. The judge asked our Foreman – have you reached the verdict? If you did, may I have it?

Foreman replied – yes your honor, we have reached the verdict. He handed the verdict paper which all of us have signed. Judge looked into the verdict and then the bailiff said – plaintiff and defendant, all rise. Everyone on both sides including us stood up, only person in the court was sitting was the Judge and he read the verdict. After reading the verdict the Judge looked at us and said – thank you very much for your help as a juror.

You are dismissed from Jury duty. You are free to go back to your regular life.

The plaintiff and her attorney were very joyful with the verdict. They thanked us and said – thank you very much. Finally I got justice for my sufferance. Wish you all the best. We came out of the court room.

It is time for us to depart from one another. Some of us developed some friendships amongst ourselves. We hugged, we exchanged telephone numbers, we wished good luck to one another, and our hearts became heavy for the ensuing painful separation. During this process we became like a family, our family broke today, we did not know if we would meet again in future, but hoped to do so. I was looking one after one was leaving me to join their families. I was looking them go, finally I started to walk towards my car, I was very happy, the burden came off my shoulder, I became a free man again to resume my life, to resume our family life where I left behind. I felt like I was a bird flying high in the sky with all the joys of freedom of my life, I embraced my usual life again. I was very glad to perform my civic duty as a Juror for helping the justice system of my newly adopted country. I stored this unique experience in the core of my heart of my soul. In my mind I thanked the Jury System for giving me the privilege of experiencing of such a unique justice system.

(Based on a true story, names are changed)

OUR NEW HOPE

———

Some newspapers printed the following news:

L AS VEGAS — Perched in his suite at a high-rise hotel overlooking the Vegas Strip, a 64-year-old retiree with no real criminal history and no known affiliations with terror groups rained bullets down into a crowd at a country music festival Sunday, killing at least 59 people and injuring hundreds more in the deadliest mass shooting in modern American history.

The attack, at least initially, was as inexplicable as it was horrifying. Law enforcement officials said they could not immediately tell what drove Stephen Paddock to fire at thousands of unsuspecting concertgoers from the 32nd floor of the Mandalay Bay Resort and Casino before killing himself.

Authorities said a sweep of law enforcement databases showed Paddock had no known run-ins with police, and — despite the Islamic State's repeated claims otherwise it has been determined that Paddock acted alone with no known ties with any terrorist organizations.

In another news a truck rams into bicycle lane in New York City and consequently killing many pedestrians and injuring many more. The driver of this truck shouted at the top of his voice "Allah Ho Akbar".

Oct. 31, 2017: Truck rams into cyclists, pedestrians in New York City

Many seriously injured.

Sept. 15, 2017: Terror on the tube Rail

At least 22 people were injured when an apparent bucket bomb exploded on a London subway, causing mass panic and flash burns.

Aug. 17, 2017: Van ramming in Barcelona

A van attack killed 14 people in Barcelona, while another person was stabbed to death by the attacker as he fled. Another attack in nearby Cambrils a day later left one dead. The attacks were claimed by ISIS.

June 3, 2017: Van ramming and stabbing in London

Seven people were killed and dozens were injured by three assailants who plowed through pedestrians on the London Bridge and stabbed revelers in Borough Market.

May 22, 2017: Outside Ariana Grande concert in Manchester, England

Ariana Grande holds a benefit concert following the attack. (The Associated Press.)

Wherever you look in the world news of mass murdering is taking place in different part of the world, namely Indonesia, Philippines, India, France, USA etc. These terrorists and murderers are coming to USA through the Southern Border between USA and Mexico. That is why President Donald Trump wants to put a wall between Mexico and USA so that human trafficking, drug trafficking, child labor and women for prostitution are not allowed to this side of USA. President Donald Trump promised this wall to the voters when he was elected to the presidency of United States America. The main obstacle for this wall is the Democratic Party. Although they have allocated billions of dollars for the same wall prior to the presidency of Donald Trump. Democratic party's only problem, they do not want that President Donald Trump gets the credit for securing the south Border, that is why the Democratic Party has created a huge road block for this President. It is nothing new that this Democratic Party never stands for the betterment of the Country, they only watch for their benefits and they are more interested in creating a huge number of dependent citizens who will always depend on the Government. They do not want any citizen to work independently for his own benefit and create wealth for others making the country great again, country safe again and would have a middle class who will flourish in every aspect of life. The irony about the wall is that the Democratic Leader Nancy Pelosi has a big wall around her home. If it does not work why she has erected the wall around her house, if walls do not work, break the wall. These leaders of the Congress and Senate are suffering from avarice and they only look for their own benefits like health insurance etc. I cannot understand why a Congressman's Health Insurance will be better than any other citizen of the country, life is always equally valuable be it the life of a Congressman or Senator or any other ordinary citizen of the country, ever body should have the same and equal opportunity. This is what the President Donald Trump wants to do for his countrymen but Democrats would not allow him to do it. For Immigration reforms, for installing the wall in Mexican Border the President was pleading for last two years but these selfish hate mongers in Congress would not allow him to do it. So, finally the President got tired of this kind of duplicity from the Democrats, he finally was compelled to shut down the Government for nonessential activities of the Federal Government. After 35 days both Democrats and Republicans came to a bipartisan agreement to find a way to resolve the Immigration and Wall issues. Now it is heard that they have reached to an agreement which will be acceptable to all three parties like, the President, Republicans and Democrats as well.

Unfortunately, even after a few meetings, the bipartisan committee did not allocate enough money for the wall in Mexican Border. Hundreds of thousands of illegal Immigrants are pouring in every day and to encounter this grave situation President Trump has rightfully declared a "National Emergency" and thereby he can transfer funds from one department to another and this way the Wall will be constructed. The promised Border Wall between Mexico and USA should be built and must be built to save the sovereignty of our beloved Nation and Country.

We, the citizens of this country should wake up in the wake of this Liberal and Socialistic Ideology of the left, their agenda, abolish ICE, implement open border policy and even kill a baby who is born normal if the mother decides not to keep the baby, they have no regards for the life of a human being. As a free citizen of the greatest country we have to decide now, do we want this autocratic injustice to continue or bring common sense to value the human life? Are we as a nation want our country to be ruled by anarchy and lawlessness, should we give up our human values to bunch of thugs of Democratic Party or should we embrace the life of dignity, kindness and human values that will take our country to a new height of prosperity and greatness of our nation with American values of integrity as an immigrant nation? Choice is very simple, honor and dignity of life must prevail.

We, the people of this great country, should stand behind President Donald Trump. His vision of Economic policies have brought about the lowest rate of unemployment in last fifty years, unemployment rate among Afro American is the lowest in last fifty years, while Hispanic youths are finding jobs in record numbers, salaries of women workers are catching up with their male counter parts. The Stock Market has reached record high, national GDP growth is at the highest level since last three decades, our nation has reached a new high in total assets. The country has reached a new height of wealth and prosperity under the leadership of President Donald Trump.

Week Export contracts with NAFTA, China and Canada were creating enormous dent to our economy while those countries were tremendously benefiting from this one sided deal in their favor. This was a gift from President Obama to those countries. These could lead to a criticism of President Obama's negotiating skills which have put USA in a weaker position while the other countries are in much better and stronger position economically. From day one, even before the election Donald Trump announced he will reverse from these one sided deals and as soon as he became the President, he broke those deals and made a new deal which is fair for all countries involved in NAFTA.

In 2018 midterm election, a seed of evil force was put in the land of Congress in Washington. This was done by the 5th District voters of Minnesota. Elhan Omar and this radical has emigrated from Somalia. Islamic religion is flowing through her blood which only can produce hatred for other religion and she has already started to spit the hatred when she twitted "Evil doings of Israel" It is not even one month, she is in Congress and she has started bad mouthing, now she did it against Israel, tomorrow she will do it against America. These peoples dirty their plate on which they eat their food. I assume 5th District of Minnesota has a high population of Moslems, if that is true then this District will never elect a member from other religious community, only the gender of the elected person may change to male or female but will always be a member of Islamic religion. Eventually Elhan Omar may present a bill to the Congress to implement Sharia Law in United States of America. Soon or later Minnesota's 5th District is going to look like, act like Somalia. Elhan Omar has become a member of

Foreign Relations Committee, I hope, the Democratic Party understands her bigotry and hate for other religion and condemn her for her Anti-Semitism.

These two women, Rashida Tlaib and Ilhan Omar in Congress, have planted the seed of intolerance in the country and eventually it will become a monster and will try to destroy the harmony and peace which we enjoy among peoples of different faith and religion, brotherly love and affection will vaporize due to the yearning of establishing superiority of Islamic Faith to other religious failth. In next few years the citizens of this country will feel the scorching heat of hatred spread by the intolerance of Islamic Faith and Islamization. Ilhan Omar has already put insult to injury when she said "some people did something" about the 9/11 attack where more than two thousand hard working peoples lost their lives. She has intentionally undermined the 9/11 attack to trivialize this heinous attack on innocent peoples done by the Islamic Terrorists. She holds an inherent hatred in her for the Western Civilization.

History repeats itself, it has been seen time after time in India that Moslems have betrayed the Freedom Movement of India and strengthened the hands of British Government and caused enormous damage to the country, for such action taken by some Islamic traitors, the country suffered a lot and freedom of the country was delayed a longer time. Someday, I am afraid, people of 5th District of Minnesota will regret that they sow this seed of hatred in their ground. Peoples of Islamic faith has migrated to different countries of Europe, they reside there, they work there but they always support their home country if there is a conflict of interest between their new adopted country and old country, Country of Residence always loose, does not matter how legitimate is the reason, these migrants will never embrace their newly found resident country, this is their style, this is their habit, this is what they do because this betrayal is embedded in their blood. To understand this phenomenon, look at India's Islamic population. These peoples are living in India for centuries, yet they have no loyalty for India. Majority of these Moslems have been supporting Pakistan or other Islamic Countries on a regular basis. For example when 911 happened, Moslems of Detroit and Paterson expressed their happiness by playing drums and music, similarly when Pakistani terrorists took down the Mumbai hotel by 26/11 Attack, the resident Moslems of India expressed their happiness for killing the Infidels, you cannot expect anything better from these peoples, so we as a nation should be very careful to determine who should come to our country and who should be allowed to stay in our country. Mr. President Donald Trump has the right attitude towards this problem when he restricted peoples coming to USA from certain Islamic countries. Peoples of this country should feel lucky to have a President who has real vision to solve this problem, Mr. President has rightfully decided for vetting for the potential Islamic travelers who want to enter this great country, but democrats and liberals equally wrongfully touting to keep the border open and less monitoring, this is wrong and these democrats and liberals know it, they are insisting on it just to make sure so that President Trump cannot keep his campaign promise of a secured Border between Mexico and USA.

Another ominous force came into the Congress from 14th Congressional District of New York, her name is Alexandria Ocasio-Cortez. This 29 year old woman has no idea what she talks about yet Democratic Members of the Congress has put her into the altar of their savior and started to adore her as if she is the Messiah for this no good Democratic Party. Ms. Ocasio-Cortez came up with the idea of a Green New Deal which will take some drastic measures to cut environmental pollution. In very broad strokes, the Green New Deal legislation laid out by Ocasio-Cortez and Sen. Markey sets goals for some drastic measures to cut carbon emissions across the economy, from electricity generation to transportation to agriculture. In the process, it aims to create jobs and boost the economy. This plan also propose the elimination of air plane flying with high speed train with solar power, power will be generated by wind mills, only problem poor Senator M. K. Haroon from Hawaii has already expressed her concern how she will travel to and from Hawaii to Washington D.C. These two also has proposed 70% tax from peoples worth more than 10 million dollars. By the unrealistic ideas and action of these two crazy law makers, the US Economy and Civilization will potentially walk backwards and the country will end up in a big peril of hopelessness, frustration and destruction. All these scientific inventions achieved in so many centuries and decades will fade away by the action of these unpatriotic Democratic Congress.

America is the most powerful Nation on the face of the earth. There is no power or Country which can match the military prowess of America. With its strength America has fought many wars and won them, it can still fight many more and win fighting the enemies outside the country, but how this military might is going to fight the enemies within the country? Enemies within are trying to destroy the strength of the country working under current, their silent animosity towards the country will destroy the country someday like once very powerful Roman Empire was destroyed by the enemies within. This twenty-first century may well bring an end to the Civilization of United States of America.

If anyone should be investigated, Democrats should investigate Hilary Rodham Clinton who has intentionally deleted more than thirty thousand emails from the Government Computers. She has also busted Government Computers with hammer and also has destroyed cell phones with hammer so that her wrong doings cannot be found in those devices. For any citizen it is a punishable crime when anyone destroys Government Properties. The last Hillary Clinton email dump includes one that gives away the location of U.S. Ambassador Chris Stevens, who was murdered by terrorists in Benghazi. Who is responsible for his death?

Also it is alleged that Senator Diane Feinstein's driver was a Chinese spy. This guy drove her around for last 20 years. Was he really a spy? Nobody looked into this matter. Instead of trying to depose an elected President the Democrats in Congress should investigate thoroughly about Hilary's wrong doings and Feinstein's driver's alleged spying.

If Democratic Party wants to prove their nonpartisanship, then they should immediately ask the office of the Attorney General to start investigations against Hillary Clinton for "deleting thirty thousand emails and for breaking the computers and cell phones" by hammering them, also they should ask the Attorney General to launch an investigation against Senator Diane Feinstein whose driver was an alleged Spy of China. They do not want justice, they cannot swallow the bitter pill of losing the 2016 Presidential Election to Donald Trump. Their Hillary President dream faded in the Electoral College like a camphor ball. Since then, Democrats became desperate to delegitimize the win of President Donald Trump in the last Election.

Democrats do not want this President to succeed. They are trying to minimize his capabilities by lodging many investigations against him and his family and business. Russian Collusion, investigation produced absolutely nothing, Special Counselor Robert Mueller spent so much time and money to witch hunt but came up with three guilty pleas for lying to the authorities in nonrelated affairs instead. We the citizen of this country demand an end to this witch hunt of Russian Collusion and let the President work fearlessly for the country, for the democracy and for the citizens of this great country. So far Collusion is in the dream of the hate mongers, Mueller has failed miserably in this so called Russian Collusion Investigation. Finally, Mueller handed over the investigation report to Attorney General William Barr. William Barr summarized the report in 4 pages and described there is no proof of Russian Collusion, nor does it have any proof for Obstruction of Justice. Democrats got very upset with this report. Congress men like Jerold Nadler and Adam Schiff got very disappointed with the Attorney General and they demanded that they want to see the whole report, Congressman Nadler has passed to subpoena the whole report of special Investigator Mueller. The other Congressman Adam Schiff is demanding that President Donald Trump must submit last six year's Tax Returns which were submitted to the Internal Revenue Service. Exoneration of President Trump has made the Democrat Party a Mad Dog, they will turn every stone to overthrow this President. Now the last hope of Collusion and Obstruction of Justice being disappeared, Nadler and Schiff Company is more imbued to find the President Trump guilty of Russian Collusion and Obstruction of Justice despite the fact that special Counsellor has exonerated President Trump against all the absurd allegations. Democrats are more aggressive even more in lying and smearing against the President Donald Trump and his family. Peoples of this country feel pity for Adam Schiff and Jerold Nadler, the attack dogs of Democratic Party.

But America has hope, America has Mr. Donald J Trump as the President of United States of America. Mr. Trump is a true patriot and he wants to put USA in the highest altar of world so that America becomes the greatest country again, this is his dream and this is what he will achieve for his countrymen and his future generation. President Donald, with the help and support of his countrymen, is determined to put America first and make America Great Again. Mr. Donald Trump will remove the terrorists and news headlines caused by them. His hard work and firm standing against terrorism will never give those news headlines which we have seen in the beginning of this article. His economic policy is taking our economy to a new higher level where middle class America will expand and poverty in America will diminish and decrease to a great extent. Under his presidency Middle Class America is dreaming again for financial and social success.

President Trump, you are our last hope, only under your leadership America will thrive again, America will be great again, and together we shall make America Great again.

OUR LABOR DAY

—

Every year winter drags on, it feels like winter is never ending. However, eventually it comes to an end. Everybody is very happy, heavy bundling up becomes history, finally warm weather arrives, summer days start to roll, hot and humid days reign and peoples start to think when this summer will leave. We all wait for this time of the year when temperature will be moderate and days will be pleasing and enjoyable. Announcement of Labor Day makes me nervous, because it implies that summer is over and winter days are not far behind. Peoples start to think how they are going to spend the Labor Day. Normally peoples invite their friends and family and do barbecue in their back yard and enjoy the food they prepare. In the past we have spent the Labor Day as any American family would, invite friends and family, barbecue chicken and vegetables and enjoy them. But this year we had no plan at all. As a family we had no plan how to spend the Labor Day. In the past years we never had any plan for it. This year was not different either. We did not have any plan whatsoever. Normally, I play tennis in the morning with my buddies. So, I got up early and went to tennis court around seven in the morning. While I was driving towards the court, I heard the phone ringing, I picked up the phone and was surprised to hear the most beautiful voice of the whole world; it was none other than my beloved daughter, Krista. She smilingly said – dad, good morning, what are you doing?

Knowing her a late riser, I was worried a bit and anxiously asked her – are you guys alright? You are up so early, what makes you get up this time of the morning.

She said – dad, I hear wind, are you driving?

I said – yes, I am driving and going to play tennis, wish me luck. We always joke, my daughter would ask me, how I did in the game. I would always reply – my partner was terrible and if he would have played a little better we could win the set. My daughter would smile at me and say – ye dad, I am waiting to hear from you that you played bad, and you lost, don't blame your partner, give him credit, he tried his best and admit your opponent played very well. We joke about it. She smiles, I smile and we laugh about my tennis game. She said – dad, when are you coming back home?

May be around 10 o'clock, do you need me for doing anything? I replied to her. Since I am retired and do not have a regular routine of life, I am the one who fill in whenever they need do anything. It is kind of a spare tire; fit whenever and wherever they place and keep going. I do not complain about it, on the other hand I am very happy that I am still doing something for my child and family. My daughter Krista said – dad, we are thinking that if mom and you can come to our place around 11 o'clock, mom and I can walk in Central Park; Nick and you can ride bicycle, what you say? Nick is our son-in-law, he is like our son, we love him very much. I always like to do things with him. It gives me a feeling that I am doing things with my son. Nick wants to ride bicycle with me in Manhattan; that is the best thing we can do together. I would not miss it even for the world. So without giving any second thought I replied – ma, we are coming. Did you ask your mom? Please tell her I will be home by 10 o'clock. See you later alligator.

She smiled and replied – alright Biluda. She hanged up the phone. Whenever she is very happy with me, instead of calling me dad, she calls me Biluda. Her mom and I always enjoy whenever she calls me Biluda. We love to see our daughter happy and content. Every parent do. I know that our sweet heart was going to call her mom now and we are going to Manhattan this morning to her home, our sweetie pie's home.

Our daughter got married about three years back. They live in midtown Manhattan. Their apartment is small but enough for two of them. It is a one bed room apartment. When you enter the apartment, kitchen is in your left, bed room is on your right and the living is straight ahead. It is on a high floor. All you can see is the upper floors of other buildings and some roads far beyond, there you see peoples are wandering but their sizes look small, sometimes you may feel whole road is filled with small men and women; may remind you Gulliver's travel's Island where men and women were all very small, may be a few inches tall. Anyway, we like their cozy home, especially their warmth of caring, love and affection for us, make us feel that we are their small children and they are our parents. Our son-in-law Nick said to my wife – ma, would you like to have some coffee. He knows she likes the coffee when he makes it. For me, I am really not a coffee person. Glass of diet coke is good for me and Nick knows it. He has already brought me a glass of diet coke. I took a sip from the glass. Nick started to make coffee. My wife and daughter started to chat, nothing special, usual mother daughter talk. Nick knows she like black coffee without sugar.

Nick came to the living room with two cups of coffee, one for him and one for his Ma (mother-in-law). Our daughter said – Nick, dad and you ride the bicycle, ma and I will walk around the Central Park in the walkway. Make sure you keep an eye on dad because he did not ride a bicycle in the recent past. It's been a while since he rode a bicycle. His balance might have been reduced due to non-practice. She expressed her fears about my riding trip with Nick.

Krista, two things peoples do not forget in life, one is swimming, the other is riding a bicycle, once you learn them, you never forget them, only your skill may be little rusty, if I fall I will get up it's not a big deal, so, don't worry your Biluda will be fine. Neither I forgot how to ride a bicycle nor will I ever. I shall be able to ride a bicycle as long as I can stand up. Do not be worried, my bicycle trip will be real good, especially when father son teamed up in this. – I assured her. Once I finished talking her mother said-Krista, don't bother my husband, he should be okay. My wife smiled at her with her usual affection.

Krista said – Ma, your husband is a stubborn man, he does not want to admit that he is ripe now, he has limitations, besides a few months ago, remember, he had an episode of orthostatic hypertension, besides dad always complains about his knees now a days. Bicycle pedaling needs lot of knee work. Then looked at me stopped. My daughter never calls me old, she always calls me ripe. Her way of denying that day by day I am growing old. Occasionally she will tell me – dad, I am very glad that you like outdoor activities, tennis, etc. I always tell my friends that my father is very athletic, he does things which a person of his age will never try to do. Please be careful, I want you to have fun not get hurt. After finishing her speech, she hugged me and said – okay Biluda, let us go downstairs and start our walk and you two start your bike riding. I was thinking how mature she acts now a days. I remembered those days when she was a little girl, how lively she was, when I would come from work, as soon she saw me she would come running to my lap; hardly ever I would get a chance to put my bag down before I realized she would cling to my waist. I remembered when I used to take her out every Wednesday in the summer; we would wander around the shopping mall, from store to store, my rule was very clear, you can touch any toy but you have put it back wherever it belonged; then we would have lunch in McDonald's, because that was her favorite food. Once in a while I would buy her a toy and we would come home before her mom came back from her work. My little girl is a grown up person, I do not have the luxury of taking her out anymore, she has a life of her own with her husband, whenever I have free time for myself I try to walk through the memory lane of yesterday where she was still my little girl, just a daddy's girl. I came back to my senses when I heard the voice of my wife – stop daydreaming, we are going for walk from here, Nick and you go for your trip. We shall meet you somewhere between 2 and 2:30 in the afternoon. Then she turned towards my daughter and said – Krista, let's go. They started to walk towards Central Park. I said to both of them – have fun, see you later.

Nick told me – dad, let's go to a Citibike stand. It is only a Block away. We started to walk towards the bike stand. About two years back, Mayor Bloomberg has started a program called "Citibike". They have installed hundreds stands where you can rent a bicycle for five dollars. Nick has a card which he uses to rent the bike. He loves to ride bicycles, so do I, only difference he rides it regularly, I did not ride for last few years. I am little nervous, because of lack of practice, the other reason is for riding the bike in the city streets which is full of peoples, cars and travelers from different countries. Combination of all of these were the reasons of my worries. I expressed my anxiety to Nick – are we going to ride in 8th Avenue? It is very busy now, lots of people are walking, it is kind of busy, have to be very careful.

No, dad, we are not going through 8th Avenue, we may go through this avenue, may be for four or five blocks. After that we shall go to Central Park bike lane and ride the bike- Nick stopped. Then he said – don't worry, we will be fine. He tried to assure me. In the meantime, we have taken two bikes from the bike stand. Nick paid for it. The he lowered the seat for me. Then he explained the route we were taking for the central park. Nick said – dad, you go first, go slow, I shall be following you. We entered into Central Park through 59th street and 8th avenue gate. We approached the bicycle lane very slowly because a large number of pedestrians were wandering aimlessly enjoying the sunshine, enjoying close relationship of family and friends. It seemed to me that everyone was in a joyful mood, trying to spend their time as lazily as possible. We did not ride through this crowd, we walked slowly through them. Finally we reached the bike lane. Nick explained to me that bike lane follows the same traffic rules as the cars. If there is a red light, we have to stop for the pedestrians etc. I knew these traffic rules. But I was amazed to see that Nick was trying to teach me in a way as if I was a little boy. I was overwhelmed by his caring and I thanked God that we have a son-in-law who is such a loving and caring person. In my mind I thanked God for having him in our family. We circled around the Central Park for a few times, I don't exactly remember how many times, but it must be three or four times. At the end of the last lap Nick told me – dad, we have finished riding in Central Park, now we shall go to the riverside bike ride lane. When we go to the gate at 8th Ave and 60th Street, we shall get out of the Park and we shall go start for the Riverside Bike Lane, we shall take 58 Street and go towards west, towards Hudson River bank where we shall ride by the side of the river.

"Alright Nick, I will stop when I come there" – I told Nick. Anyway I was feeling little tired and I thought this stop will give a chance to take a breath and reenergize me for the Riverside Bike Lane. I was having real good time with that Citibike. Although once in a while I wanted ride a bicycle in Manhattan, in my entire life, I never thought that I would be ever riding a bicycle in Manhattan, my dreams would come true in a better way that I would be riding with my dear son-in-law, Nick. God has unique way of rewarding people, I felt I was one of those lucky ones who had the luxury fulfilled dreams. Silently I expressed my gratitude to the Almighty.

We started to ride from the corner of 8th Ave and 60th street and started going towards south traveling through 8th Avenue. This riding was not bad because they have designated bicycle land where a cyclist can ride very safely. Mayor of the city has done a great thing, he has created all these bicycle lanes for the bicyclists. I think, the mayor himself was a fan of bicycle riding, whatever may be the case, has done a great service to the bicycle riders. Now any tourist can rent a bicycle and see the city his way and have fun. This was not available in New York City before, before Subway or Cabs were the ways of traveling; not any more, now bicycle has added the freedom to any traveler. Riding a bicycle through bike lane of any avenue is safe but riding through any street is quite different; a cyclist has to be a real careful rider because there is no bike lane and streets are like jungles filled with cars, cab and buses; everyone is trying to beat everyone; cab drivers of this city are famous for their aggressive driving, they don't care, they just want to go, does not matter how. Traffic rules and disciplined driving are hardly followed there, so any bicyclist has to be extra careful for riding his bike; accidents may happen any second. We were riding through a street going towards south for going to the bank of Hudson River. It was downhill, it felt great, bike was going faster and faster, it was not a problem for me, suddenly

I realized that traffic light is red and I have to stop, my speed gave some trouble but I managed to stop without any incident. After passing this light we came to the famous bicycle lane of Hudson River. This lane starts from North and goes all the way to the Battery Tunnel, quite a few miles, I do not exactly how many mile. It was exciting enough for me that I was going to ride bicycle by the side of the famous Hudson River. Nick said to me "dad, look on the other side of the river, that is the Jersey City."

I looked on the other side of the river, it was beautiful, Jersey's buildings were looking very bright because sunlight shone them, rays of sun were coming from some of the buildings, it was spectacular, I felt very lucky that I could become a witness of such a beauty of nature and human creation of architectural beauty as well. Nick said – dad, we shall towards south a few miles then we shall return, if you feel tired, let me know, we shall go back at that time, you are riding a lot today, make sure your legs do not cramp. I heard concern in his voice about my health.

I told him – Nick, don't worry whenever I feel tired I will stop. And we will go back.

Nick said –dad, I know, you play tennis a lot, your physical activities are praiseworthy but I still wanted to let you know that whenever you want to stop; we will stop and go back. Now let us go. We started riding by the side of the Hudson River, a lifetime experience for me. I felt, I am very lucky to gain an experience like this, especially when I am having this experience with my son-in-law, Nick. Very few people has luck to do things together with son-in-law. We were going up and down the lane, after about half an hour, Nick stopped and asked me to stop. He said – Krista called me, they are waiting for us, I think we should go back now. They are ready for lunch. Do you want to ride more, or should I tell her that we are coming?

Yes, tell them, we are coming – I told Nick. We stopped and started to go back.

dad, we are going to take 48 Street, all the other streets are uphill; 48 Street will be easy for us because it is more flat than any other streets around here, your knees won't have to work heard – Nick told me. I was glad to hear him because I did not want to go uphill, I was afraid my knees might hurt, once again it made me happy that he always thinks about my comfort and safety.

Nick, where are we going to meet them – I asked him.

In the corner of 50th Street and 8th Avenue – Nick replied. We started rolling and in about fifteen minutes we reached the corner of meeting place. Krista and her mom were sitting on a bench. They saw us and stood up to greet us. My wife said – how far did you guys go, it's been so long that you two were gone. Then she looked at me and said – I hope your knees do not give you pain. I hope you are happy now that you rode in Manhattan, and that too with Nick, your dream came true, right. Nick, did he bother you? - She wanted to know.

Nick was smiling, then he said – Ma, no he did not bother me, he bothered other bikers, they were afraid of dad. He joked about my riding. Then he said – no Ma, dad was a perfect responsible biker. I am very glad that we both rode together, I will remember it all my life. Then he looked at Krista and said – where are going to have lunch?

Krista looked at me and said – Biluda, how was it, are you tired? Then looked at Nick and said – we are going to have lunch in Renaissance Restaurant.

Krista, I am hungry, let's go to the restaurant, I will tell you about my ride when we sit for the lunch – I replied her.

Nick said – Krista, let us walk to the restaurant. I guess everybody is hungry by this time. We shall talk when we sit there in the restaurant. Finally we reach the restaurant. We sat on a table outside under a tent which is kind of open, sunny and was very pleasing with light breeze. The waitress gave us some water, everyone drank some water, Nick and I ordered two bottles of beer. Krista and her mom ordered some diet coke. She gave us some time to look into the menu. Krista asked me – Biluda, how does it feel to ride a bicycle in Manhattan? She looked at me with her happy smile. I looked at my daughter and said – it was great, I felt great and my dream was fulfilled today, so I am very happy and content about it; now Nick can tell you how I did in riding. Nick gets the credit for the experience which I got today because he is the one who guided me in the whole bicycle route, he guarded me like a father who guards his young son. I looked at Nick and said – Nick, thank you very much for being my dad on the road. He did not reply, he gave his usual charming smile. In the meantime, food came on the table and we started to get busy with delicious looking foods. Krista's mom said – this fish is delicious, Krista, do you want a small bite? We shared our food with one another. I asked Krista – how was your mother daughter time, anything special happened, we should know. Krista smiled and said – no, Biluda, nothing special. Ma bought me this necklace from the roadside stall. It is so pretty. Dad, do you like it? She stopped. I noticed it too. Nick smiled and told – dad, she got the necklace from mom, what do I get from you? My answer to him was very simple and small – Nick, of course, you get this for helping me in riding. I handed him the restaurant bill for payment. But to my surprise, this bill was paid earlier by our daughter, Krista. Nick was perplexed, at a loss what to do, we all started laughing and Nick said – well my turn is next. We all stood up to return to our daughter's apartment, I realized, together with our daughter and son-in-law we finished a very happy day, this year's Labor Day.

OUR AUNTIE SUCHITRA

—

L ate forties of last century India was fully in political turmoil in which many families like this Banerjee family was devasted by the impact of division of the one country into two creating 'Hindustan and Pakistan" on the basis of Religion. But this story did not start after the partition of the country, it rather started many years ago before this political division. However, later on this family could not save itself from the perils of this partition but that is a different story. This Banerjee family was a family in a village of Mymensingh District, the family used to own many acres of land and the primary income of this family used to come from the cultivation of these lands. Family was self-sufficient from this income in every way of life. The head of the family was Debdas Banerjee who could not finish his high school because he joined the country's independence movement while he was in grade tenth, he was hiding from the British Rulers and went to jail a few times for his active participation in this movement. By the time he became an adult he found that his father passed away, his elder sister Suchitra who was twelve years older than him has come to her father's house after her husband passed away from a heart attack. In this situation he took the charge of the family and decided to help the freedom movement by staying with the family. The twenties of last century was the peak of freedom movement, the Non-cooperation movement was launched on 5th September, 1920 by Mahatma Gandhi with the aim of self-governance and obtaining full independence as the Indian National Congress withdrew its support for British reforms following the Rowlatt Act of 21 March 1919, and the Jallianwala Bagh massacre of 13 April 1919, the country was burning like a fire ball in the explosion of dissatisfaction for the act of British Rulers and its far reaching effect reached every family of India at that time.

Around this time Suchitra came back to stay forever with her father after losing her husband in a heart attack. Her husband's family did not want to share the property with her, so they throw her out of the house and sent her to her father's house. Suchitra was only twenty years old and she had a baby daughter to take care. **In this situation she had no place to go but to her father.** Her father embraced this unlucky daughter and since then she became a part of her father's family. Few years later her father also passed away suffering from some unknown malady. Suchitra and her brother lost their father and their mother also passed away many years before that. Since then as an elder sister Suchitra took charge of the family and Deb started to look after their family farming business. Although she did not have her husband life was good for her living in her father's house. She forgot the pain of losing a husband with the love of daughter and brother's affection and care. Although she had some importunity in her, she also had the sense to eliminate them from her daily life. Unfortunately, at that time she lost her two years old daughter who was suffering from the disease of Typhoid. Firstly, she lost her husband, now the only child, it was a deadly blow in her life. Her happiness disappeared like a camphor ball. She started to live the life a sad widow. She started to take resort to God and gradually devoted her life to their family temple serving the God. Then one day she told her brother – Deb, I think you should get married now, it is becoming difficult for me to take care of the family and the temple.

Debu listened to her sister and said – Didi (big sister), we have so many helping hands, ask them to do the chores, they will do them for you. You don't have to work hard. Okay I shall ask them to help you.

Suchitra embraced her brother with affection and said – brother, that is not the point, I need to see my brother got settled in life, if something happens to me, I want to make sure that there is someone who will take care of you. Now, if you agree with me, I shall ask the family matchmaker to find a beautiful bride for you. So, I am going to ask our family matchmaker Parimal Babu to see me.

Deb's face became red with shyness, somehow, he nodded his head and said – Didi, I don't know, do whatever you think is right.

Few months later Deb got married to Anita with a festival like ceremony. All the villagers were invited in the wedding. Both Deb and Anita have settled down after the jovial ceremony of wedding. Little by little Anita was being introduced to the family chores and Suchitra and Anita started to become more friendly with one another. Before Anita's marriage Suchitra explained to her the family situation and also mentioned that Anita has to take care of the family's reputation and integrity. Anita was an autodidact very smart girl, she understood the dynamics of this well to do family, the ideals and devotion for God were already inculcated in her by her parents. She also understood the curse of being a widow at an early age. She fully understood the ins and outs of the life of a young woman who lost everything at a young age, the loneliness, the pain and the agony which a widow encounters were very well known to Anita, so with her compassion and empathy, very soon Anita won the mind and heart of the whole family and her husband. Since Anita came to the family Suchitra started to shy away from daily family affairs and started to devote her mind and soul to God and the family temple which was the pride of their ancestors for many years because there was a here say Lords Narayan and Krishna were very much live in this temple and if anybody desired anything from them with real respect and devotion, Lords Narayan and Krishna would grant him that as a boon. She started to find peace and happiness by praying to Lord Narayan and Lord Krishna of their temple. In the meantime, Anita learnt everything about this family and gradually she took over the daily business of running the kitchen and family. One day Anita came to this family as Deb's newly wedded bride and now she is the head of the family and she decides the daily chores and she deploys the family helping hands who will do what. During this new phase of Anita's life Suchitra guided her to the position of family's decision maker.

Eventually Anita, a siter-in-law, brother's wife became a little sister to Suchitra, Anita also started to love and respect Suchitra as her elder sister. Life was good for Anita and Suchitra, they became very tight friends, in house hold chores they both walked in different path, Anita for the family and Suchitra for the temple and religion. They both walked in parallel ways like a railway track, both going to the same destination but never meet together, they respected each other, loved each other like sisters, happiness was overflowing in the family. Anita and Suchitra always had lunch together and they would discuss different family issues during that period, they would ask the opinion of one another during that time and never criticize one another for any wrong doing, they would never cross the limit or encroach one another's space, such was the respect, love and affection for one another. In the meantime, Anita and Debu had two children, a boy and a girl, family was very happy with the new comers. One day during the lunch Anita told Suchitra – "Didi, I have given birth to these children but I request you to raise them with your love and affection, I know, you will instill the religious values and discipline in them so that someday they become very good human beings, from now on I shall become a mother to them and you will become a real mother by nurturing them potentially to their highest level of humanity."

After listening to Anita, Suchitra said – "of course, they are our blood and future, I shall always try to teach them right from the wrong, from discipline to religion, they will be the best nephew and niece of mine, I shall make sure that they always get our support when they are growing, you and I will do whatever is good for them. We shall raise them together; you will be their mother and I shall become their Auntie." By this time, they finished the lunch and discussion and both went to finish their own chores for the family. Deb's family always circled around these two women, a combination of sister and wife. They were the flesh and blood, heart and soul of Deb's family.

Then came the storm of partition in which Deb's family, like many others, became a victim of minacious atrocities done by Moslems and the then riot of Hindu and Moslem broke out, since his property fell in Pakistan Moslems threatened to kill the family if he did not move out within twenty-four hours. Having a deadly threat like that Deb had no choice but to leave the place and moved to Kolkata and as a result he lost everything and became a pauper, his financial status came down to nothing. In twenty-four hours, this family's life changed from well to do family to a destitute family, this happened as a result of an ominous partition of a country on the basis of religion. Deb's family started to sink in the deluge of poverty and partition of the country. India became free from British Rules by victimizing millions of families on both sides to the hands of perilous and religious mayhem.

It is said that misfortune never comes alone, firstly Deb's family was uprooted, then suddenly Deb's wife Anita got ill with Meningitis and as a result of this disease she passed away in a local hospital. Deb lost his wife; children lost their mother and Suchitra lost her brother's wife who was a friend and a little sister to her. Family started a journey in a stormy ocean of poverty, uncertainty and all kinds of misfortune, anyone can imagine.

Did not matter how difficult it was life went on, time passed on and stormy days or night always comes to an end. Deb's family also went through nightmares, unhappiness and so many other perilous things but Deb and his sister never lost faith in God and they always believed that they will reach the shore of happiness, sufferings are going to end soon with a bright sunshine where will be nothing but only the happiness for which they were struggling for so long.

Every night ends with day. Finally, Deb's family's sufferings started to fade away. Children finished their education. Now, since they finished their professional education, they started to find employments with good salary and benefits. One joined a Government job which provided him with a decent living quarters, he moved the family with him in his quarters. Eventually all of them found decent jobs and all of them started to support the family's finances. The eldest son moved to USA and gradually he sponsored all his brothers and sisters. Eventually all the children moved to USA except the elder daughter. She got married and started to live with her husband nearby so that she could look after her auntie and father.

In a few years Deb's family established themselves as an upper middleclass family. Every child of the family loved their Aunt Suchitra. Sometimes, Suchitra looks at them and thinks – hopefully, she raised the children the way Anita dreamt of them to be raised. Even after so many years went by after Anita's demise, there was not a single day when Suchitra did not think about her sister-in-law, Anita. She would cry in the middle of night remembering Anita but never mention Anita in front of the children because children may be upset thinking about their mother. For Deb, he lost his wife, a friend who was always there to support him. Morose took over his mind, he always missed his wife and eventually became depressed and started to smoke heavily. His smoking eventually brought about the lung cancer in him. Brother Deb and Sister Suchitra started to live alone, all the children supported their father and aunt with money and all the amenities of life for them. Children were very responsible towards their father and aunt. Deb's condition of cancer started to worsen as time passed by and he finally succumbed to the disease leaving behind his elder sister and the children. Deb's death put Suchitra in deep grief and regret thinking that although his brother was younger than her, he had to go, God could give her life to his brother and keep him alive for the sake of the children. For many days she could not sleep or eat anything by dint of this incident. With Deb's passing away Suchitra entered into a different phase of life. So long she was the head of the family but now the children came in the forefront and she did not know how the attitude of the children would be towards her. After Deb's death, some of the children rushed to home to perform the last rituals called Shraddha Ceremony.

After the consummation of the Shraddha Ceremony, all the children sat down with their aunt Suchitra, she said – Auntie, we have lost our mother many years back, we never felt that we do not have our mother, you took her place and raised us as your own children. All of us are grateful to you for this. Now we lost our father, we know you will be there for us, someday you will take our father's place. Please stay healthy and do not make us lose you, without you we will not be able to survive, we need your advice and love in every sphere of our lives. You have been the axis of this Deb family and we cannot survive without your support, love, affection and guidance because we are your children, our lives are enriched today because of your teachings, all of us are respectable part of the society because of your hard work and guidance for us. We love you, auntie, please do no become sad, we want you to see happy and joyful again.

Aunt Suchitra listened to the children and embraced all of them and said – "I am very grateful to God and also to your mother because your mother believed in me with her greatest treasures, her children. I worked extra hard for your comfort and well being so that you can grow up decently. The rest of the credit goes to you all, you worked hard, you did not mess up your life mixing with wrong crowd, you sowed the right seed now you are reaping the benefit of your sincerity, tenacity and desire to succeed. It is you who did the miracle not me, I just gave you company when you were studying and needed me. I am very proud of you all. I know – your mother is always watching your success from heaven." She stopped, she was happy, we could see the hidden happiness in her face.

At that time our elder sister said – "Auntie, some of my friends have their Aunties living in their family, and they tell me that their mom and Aunt never get along, there is always some altercations with their mom and Aunt. Please forgive me if I offend you, I am curious, mom and you ever had any argument over anything, please tell us about that." Our sister had a naughty smile in her face.

Auntie heard what my elder sister said. Then she said – "Your mother was more of my little sister than my sister-in-law. When two sisters love one another, they do not fight or argue, they support each other for every aspect of the family. We had a real sororal relation with one another." She stopped and then said – "You children are getting naughty now, you guys are trying to pull my leg. Your mother was too good to argue with. She was a very goodhearted woman. I am going to cite an example of her goodness, all the kids of the neighborhood used to call your mom "Auntie" and often some of the would come back from school straight to your mother and say – "Auntie, I am hungry, please give me something to eat. They loved her so much that they would not hesitate to ask her for food. This was your mother, how can you not like and love a person like her, young or old everyone loved her." Her voice was heavy and eyes became watery when she was telling us about our mother.

When she stopped all of us gracefully said – "Auntie, we want Prasad from you tomorrow". Since our childhood we were sitting around her when she would have her lunch. Then she would mix rice and vegetables together and make round balls of that mixture and give those balls to each of us. We were eating those balls to our hearts content. We used to call this ball "Prasad". She happily agreed with our request for tomorrow.

One day after lunch I was feeling sleepy and I decided to take a nap. When I woke up, I saw that my Auntie was making Roti, I asked my Auntie – "Why are you making Roti when Rama is here to cook for you?'

She looked at me and whispered to me – "Be quiet, Rama is sleeping, if she hears any noise, she will be very upset. She does not work at night because she watches Serials, so I make the breads at late afternoon. If she wakes up, she will start arguing with me. And also, she will quit the job leaving me alone. She always threats me like that."

I was very shocked and upset to hear it. Immediately I waked Rama up from her sleep and asked – "Do you know why you are here? You are working for our family for so many years, we treat you like our family and yet you put our Auntie to cook, you have no conscience that you are putting an old person to work and you are sleeping, shame on you. I was very upset with her. After this incident, I thought – I should take auntie to USA. But to get a visa for her would be difficult, she could get a visa for only for six months, that is not going to solve the problem. Also, auntie told me that she will not go to USA. Our other option was that if Auntie lives in my sister's house then all the troubles will be over and my sister can take care of her. That afternoon I went to my sister's house and described what Rama was doing to our Auntie and asked if she would be able to keep her in her house. When I finished – my sister said "I would be delighted to look after her. We have so many vacant rooms in the house, Auntie can stay wherever she wants to stay. Before I came back to USA, I shifted our Auntie to our sister's home. I wanted to let Rama go but Rama apologized and started to cry that she has no place to go. Listening to her our Auntie forgave her and told me that a good-looking young woman like her may fall victim in the hands of rogue peoples and told me – "son, forgive her this time. Besides your sister will keep an eye on her if she does not behave well." I found our kind hearted Auntie once again, who felt for other's distress and helplessness. I warned Rama and arranged for the shifting before I came back to USA. My sister made complete separate living arrangement for my Auntie so that our Auntie can live very comfortably in her own way with her Lord Krishna and Lord Narayan. Whenever we visited her, our daughter would spend all of her times with my Auntie, she would not go to visit any place without her "Didimoni" which she used to call my Auntie. My Auntie lived with my sister for many years until she passed away in December of 1993.

Few years later at the request of the Authority of the high School (which I attended) I rebuilt all the edifices of the school. When the new rebuilt school was opened, the School Authority wanted to dedicate one of the School Buildings in the name of a person whomever I wanted to dedicate. I was very delighted with this proposal of the School and later on my sister and I decided that I shall dedicate the library building in the name of Auntie as she always loved children and she always encouraged us to study. I thought, this way her soul will always be with children and she will always be around them when they study. Upon our desire, the School Authority named the Library Building as "Suchitra Path Bhaban" (in Bengali "সুচিত্রা পাঠভবন"). Since then whenever I visit India, I always visit the "Suchitra Path Bhaban" where my Auntie will remain alive happily forever. Since then whenever I visit this "Suchitra Path Bhaban", I can feel that our auntie is showering her blessings on all of us with her deep love and affection.

POCKET MAAR

—

In my early years we lived in a place called Patipukur. In a small house, my family rented a room. The walls were made of mud. Basically it was a slum. Very poor people used to live in that neighborhood. We were one of the families who lived there. I was about twelve years old. For the first time I came to Kolkata. Before that I was living in a remote village which was about a hundred mile from this place. I was a village kid. Never been in a city before. It was hard for me to keep up with the neighborhood kids. Some of them were very cunning. When I came there for the first time, I was admitted to the local school in 8th Grade. I was new in school. After 6th grade, I did not have a chance to go to 7th grade. Skipping of one year of class in school put me behind. I did not know the stuff which was taught in 7th grade. I was working hard to catch up with rest of the class. It was not bad for subjects other than Math. In math, a year's absence made a huge difference. At that time algebra was taught in 7th grade. I missed that part completely. I did not know anything about algebra. My focus became to learn about algebra. I needed some coaching. We did not have money to hire a tutor. So, I was looking for somebody who was going to higher class and good in algebra and be willing to teach. Normally a student would not charge any money for helping. So, I was looking for a person like that. Finally, I found somebody whose name was Binoy. Binoy was a good student and was going in 10th grade. One of my class teachers introduced me to him and asked Binoy if he could help me out with my algebra. Binoy agreed and said – I will be more than happy to help him. But he has to come to my house at my time. That was not a problem for me. I agreed with him and set a starting date for this tutoring.

I was going to Binoy's house every other day. He was a good tutor. I was learning from him and practicing algebra every day at home. Within a very short period of time my progress was up to the class. My hard work and dedication paid me off. In fact my progress was so good that in half yearly examination, I scored the highest marks in many subjects including mathematics. All the teachers started to recognize me as a potential good student. Now lot of classmates were asking me about home work and stuff. In my class there were two students who drew my attention. One was known as Amal. The second one was known as Mantu. Amal was always in good cloths. He was well groomed child. The other drew my attention because he used to spend money for his friends. Amal and Mantu were very good friends. Later on I came to know they used to go to movies together. But their class work was not good. Probably were not studying enough. One day both of them came to me and said – Will you come with us in the lunch time? We shall have some food from the restaurant close by.

I said – "I do not have any money for the restaurant. Besides, I have to go home, my mom will be waiting for me. I shall eat at home. You two go."

Mantu said – "you don't have to spend any money. I have money. You are coming with us."

"No, I am not. I have to go home." I was firm in my point.

"Will you come after the school with us?" Amal and Mantu backed off.

"No, I cannot. I have other things to do at home. May be some other time." I was firm on my point.

Couple of days later, during the lunch time we were playing in the school ground. Amal and Mantu also joined us. We were playing with marble balls. At the end Mantu asked me – "will you help me in doing my summer home work?" Because school was going on summer vacation in next seven days. During the summer they were giving us home work. At the end we have to give them to the teachers. We had homework mostly English, Bengali and Mathematics. Some time Sanskrit too.

"I can do that. But I have to come to your house because we live in a very small place."

"No, problem. We can study in our house." Amal said.

"Then we shall study together but no fooling around" – I told them. I knew my mother always told me ' education is the most important thing in my life.' I did not want anybody to jeopardize my education. I made it very clear to them. They agreed. I agreed. I told my mom that Amal and Mantu would be my study partners in the coming summer. I also let my mother know that I like them. I wanted to be their friend.

Besides, I felt some body needed me. That was a good feeling. Although I was very young, I knew what exactly I wanted. I knew, my mom always trusted me. Up to that point I always spoke her the truth. If I could not speak the truth I would try to be quiet. But she would make me speak the truth any way. She had her ways of finding the truth. My feelings for mom were very intense. I loved her too much to disappoint her. I always tried my best to satisfy her wishes. I wanted to be an ideal son. A good son.

After a week our school had summer vacation. We all had our home works for the summer. In English, Bengali and Mathematics. My goal was to finish the home work in two weeks. After that I would work on my other projects. I always liked to finish the job first then fool around with my time. As soon as the vacation started I decided to finish the home work first then play or do whatever I liked. When Mantu and Amal asked me if they could do home work with me. I told them – "I can work with you but no wasting of time. I want to finish my home work in two weeks. If you can agree with me, you are welcome to study with me. Otherwise I cannot."

"We shall be happy to work with you. You finish the mathematics first then we shall copy them. That way nobody is going to bother you." Was Amal's idea.

"That is alright with me." We made a gentleman's agreement.

Since we lived in a very small place, I use to go to Mantu's or Amal's house for doing the home works. Mantu's mother passed away when he was five or six years old. His grand mother, father's mother, was raising him. His father did not marry again.

He was the only child. His grandmother gave him love and enough indulgence as well. She never said no to him. Whatever he wanted from his grandmother, he always got it. Whether it is money or toys, she would give him no matter what. Mantu would manipulate her to his benefit. His mind was not in school. Not in studies. He loved to watch movies. Sometimes he would not come to school. You could see him in movie halls. He knew all the names of heroes and heroins of movie world. I did not see a movie yet. My knowledge about movies was practically nil. All I have seen was the advertisements of movies. Never been to a cinema hall. It did not attract me either for some reason. Amal was a different story. His parents were alive. His mother was a wonderful lady. Whenever I went to her house, she always offered me some food. Besides she was very affectionate. His father was a goldsmith. They had their own business. His father was a very joyful and happy person. They both were kind of happy because I was hanging around their son. They thought if I hanged around their son, he would put his mind in school too. Amal's mother always asked me to study in her house with Amal. I liked Amal's mother. She was kind to me. Besides she would give me food to eat every time I went their house. That was more than enough for me to like her. When you are young, food is one of the things that you like most. I was not different either. I liked food. I liked his mother. Summer was going good. I was doing my home work with both of them. I played foot ball in their team. Both of them accepted me as a friend. Since I was new in school, their acceptance meant a lot to me. I was passing my days happily. Summer was going fast. Summer was good.

One day in the morning Mantu came to our home and asked me if I could go to his house to study. I told him I have to ask my mother. Only if she lets me go, I shall go. I asked my mother – "Ma, Can I go to Mantu's house to study. Mantu is asking me to go to his house."

"Yes. But make sure you come back before 1 o'clock".

"Yes, Ma. I will do that." I replied. Mantu and I left our home for Mantu's house.

When we came out of the house Mantu told me – "we have to go to Amal's house and ask him if he wanted to come with us." So, both of us went to Amal's house. I heard Mantu told Amal's mother that we were going to my Aunt's house in Maniktala. Amal came with us.

"Mantu, we are supposed to study. How come you told his mother that we were going to my aunt's house. I don't have an aunt in Maniktala. How come you lied to her?"

"You see this. This is why I lied to her." He took out a hundred rupee note from his pocket and showed us.

"Where did you get this money?" I asked.

"My grandmother."

"Did she give it to you?" I wanted to know.

"No, I took it from her. I asked for some money and she told me to take two rupees. But I found this bill and took it."

"What would you tell her when she finds out that you stole the money from her?"

"No, she won't find out. She has lots of them under her bed. She never keeps them counted. Don't worry she will never find out. We are going spend hundred rupees today and have good time." Saying this, he gave a cunning smile.

"I don't like it." I told Mantu. "Count me out. I am going home. You guys go." I told them.

"Bratin, nobody will know. Believe me. I did it before. My grandmother will never know. She has plenty of them. Please come for this time. I promise, I shall never ask you again." He tried to convince me to go along with the plan.

"Bratin, we have done it before. Mantu's grandmother will never find out. We did it before. Please come with us. We shall eat in a good restaurant and go to cinema." Amal pleaded to me." He was desperate. He held my hand and looked at me. Beseeching was in voice.

I knew it was wrong. I could not support them. My mind told me not to go with them. But there was a big temptation. I had never eaten in any restaurant. Never been to any movie. I was lured by them. I was not strong enough to hold my decision of not going with them. Temptation was too strong. I forgot my mother asked me to return by noon. I have never disobeyed my mother. I was allured by cinema and restaurant. I succumbed to temptation. I did not care about the consequences. Temptation took over me and finally I agreed with them.

We started to walk. At first we have to break the hundred rupee bill. We could not go to the local store owners for changing the bill. Because they would ask where did we get the money from. So, we decided to walk down to Shyambazar and break the bill there for smaller notes. It took us fifteen twenty minutes to go to Shyambazar. We tried in couple of stores.

Nobody would change it for us. Finally one store keeper agreed to change it but he wanted to keep one rupee for changing it. We gave him the bill and he returned us ninety nine rupees. We were happy to get rid of the hundred rupee note. All we needed is the change.

After changing the money we went to small snack shop. We had lassi, a yogurt drink. In the snack shop we decided to go to Esplanade, which was the heart of the city. All the actions were there. They knew it. I did not. I was following them.

We took a taxi cab. The cab driver asked – "Where you boys want to go?"

"Esplanade near Metro cinema hall." Said Mantu.

In Esplanade, we got off the taxi. We paid him the fare. I was astonished to see such a beautiful place. All the stores were very bright. Peoples were well dressed. The whole place was crowded. Everybody is walking by. Looked like everybody ignored the existence of the other person. Nobody cared about anybody. It was like a stream. It only flows and does not know how to stop. This was a unique experience for me. Specially, I was living in a village. I was a village boy. I have never been exposed to such elegance of city. I looked around. Everything was new to me. I was overwhelmed by this apparent gorgeousness of the place. Everything made me spell bound. I forgot everything. I forgot my mother told me to return before noon. I forgot that I was doing a wrong thing to spend the stolen money. Nothing mattered to me. I wanted to be there. To enjoy there. I thought, thank god, I came with them. I would have missed all these beautiful things which I saw around me if I did not come with them.

"Let us buy the tickets for this English movie." Said Mantu. We both agreed. When I used the word we, it was not really we, it was really Amal. I was kind of passive because I did not know anything about movies. But we could not buy tickets for the English movie. Because that was for adults only. Not for us kids. We were kind of disappointed for not being able to buy tickets for the English movie. We started to walk. Actually they walked. I followed. We bought some ice cream. We drank water from green coconut. We ate anything we wanted to eat on our way to the movie hall. Finally we bought three first class tickets for the movie called 'Pocket Maar'. Hero's roll was acted by Dev Anand. It was a movie in Hindi language. I forgot the name of the movie theater hall. It happened so many years ago. The movie would start at one in the afternoon. We had some time to spend. Mantu said - let us go to a restaurant. We will finish our lunch. Then we shall go to the movie. We went to a restaurant. I don't remember the name quite well, but I think it was Sabir. In the restaurant. As a first timer I did not know what to order. But my friends helped me with that. We ordered lots of food. Some we ate. Some we could not. We wasted a lot. My stomach was full. I learned the names of the dishes from them. I was like a frog from the well to the pond. Did not know what to do. Yet I enjoyed everything. I thought, thank god, I came otherwise I would have missed this fun. I did not remember my mother's order to go back before noon even for a moment. I was very much consumed by this experience.

Finally, we went to the inside of the cinema hall. They were showing all the advertisements. Some Hindi songs were being played. At the end of these, the movie ' Pocket Maar ' started. My mind sank deep in the movie. I forgot everything. All I could see is the screen in front of me.

It was two in the afternoon. My mother was worried about me. She sent my brother to Mantu's house. My brother came back and told that Mantu's grand mother told him that Mantu went to Dilip's Aunt's house. Dilip's aunt? My mother got confused because my aunt lived with us. She did not live any place else but with us. She heard and asked my brother to go to Amal's house. If Amal's mother knew anything about us. Amal's mother told the same thing that Amal and Mantu went Dilip's aunt's house. All three of them. She told my brother to ask my mother not to worry about us. We would be fine and come back home in time. She was worried about me. She knew – I was not street smart. I came from a village. It was a huge difference of life. Life styles. In the city, kids are cunning. Her son did not fit there. She became frustrated not knowing what to do. This made her angry. This kid deserved a lesson. He needed to be punished.

I enjoyed the movie very much. There were songs and dances. Of course fighting was there also. I forgot what the story of the movie was about. One thing for sure, we, all three of us, enjoyed the movie.

After the movie, we went to the Maidan which is a big field. We saw a few football matches. We finished none of them. We sat down on the ground near the monument which I saw for the first time. It was late. I realized my mother would be anxious for me. She would be worried. I decided to go home. I told Mantu and Amal – let us go home. My mother would be worried about me. It was about seven in the evening. We took a cab. We did not come to our neighborhood in the cab. We got off about a quarter of a mile away from our home. We did not want anybody to see us in the cab. That would raise many questions. We came walking to our neighborhood. Now I was coming to my house. Now I realized the gravity of the situation. My heart started to go fast. I was nervous. What am I going to tell my mother? I was scared. I knew I was in big trouble. I tried to prepare myself for the consequence. I entered the home. I could not look straight to my mother's eyes. She always taught us to look at her eyes when we spoke to her. I could not do that.

"What happened? You did not come back in time. Where did you go? Why are you so late?" Asked my mother. She had an angry look in her face. I could foresee the trouble that was coming to me.

"I went to Mantu's aunt's house" – I lied to her. For the first time in my life. My voice was weak. I was real scared.

"Oh, When did you go there? What did you eat there in lunch?" She asked. She was grave and her voice was calm. I felt this calmness was nothing but the starting of a big storm. I knew it was coming to me. I felt very guilty. I lied to her. I was looking down.

"Look at my eyes and tell me what you told me" – was her statement. She was very angry.

"Ma, I lied to you. I went to see a movie with Mantu and Amal. We ate in a restaurant. Please forgive me. I shall never do it again." I promised to her.

"Where did you get the money?" My mother wanted to know.

"Mantu got it from his grandmother." I said. My voice was very timid. I also told her that Mantu stole a hundred rupee note from his grandmother. I confessed. I became an accomplice of theft.

My mother was very angry. She asked my brother to fetch her a hand fan. At that point I knew it was coming to me. And it was coming heavy on me. My mother did a good job on me with handle of that hand fan. I was crying silently. I was enduring the beating. I deserved punishment. After a while she stopped and told – "I want to see that it never happens again. If it does, you will be dead." Remember this. Her voice was ice cold.

"Ma, I shall never let you down again." I promised to her.

After a few days, I told my mother the whole story of our movie adventure of that day. I told her the name of the movie was 'Pocket Maar'. Mantu really picked the pocket of his grandmother and with that money we have seen the movie. We also became pick pockets. All three of us. Myself, Amal and Mantu. My mother said – "I hope you got your lesson." She looked at me. I could see only love and affection in her face. I embraced her and said – "Ma, I love you. Please forgive me. I shall never do anything stupid like this anymore."

She looked into my eyes deeply to find if I was telling her the truth. I saw a smile in her eyes. I was relieved – my mother believed me. I knew she has her dreams about me. I promised to myself – I will never become a reason for her sadness. I said – Ma, please forgive me. I embraced my mother and I heard her voice – "we shall see." I knew - my mother was happy for me. I felt her love and affection wrapped me around, I felt relieved and very secured.

PROMISE

—

After my graduation from Jadavpur University I started to look for work in different pharmaceutical companies. When I studied in the university, I was working for a company. That company was one of the most stable companies in India at that time. My salary was much higher in that company than that of what I could earn as a graduate pharmacist. My family was mostly dependent on me. So I decided to keep my old job unless I can get a job which will give me at least the same salary. So, I would routinely look into the wanted column on Sunday's The Statesman and The Amritabazar Patrika. Every week I was applying for new job to 2 or 3 companies. One of my engineer friends once told me that his friend was going to America for employment. He told me – Dilip, I shall introduce you to him and you can ask him what to do to go to America. The conversation ended there. I completely forgot about it. Occasionally I used to meet my old classmates share ideas and information. One day I went to see my friend Subhankar in Jadavpur and after lunch we decided to go to a movie. We decided to go to Esplanade and watch any English movie. We got on an 8B bus. Luckily we found room to sit. As soon as we settled down Subhankar said – Dilip, I heard America needs professionals like doctor, engineer, and pharmacist and so on and they are granting permanent resident ship to those peoples. I am thinking of going to American Consulate one day and find out about it.

I said – why one day, why not now? Let us get off at the next stop and go to American Consulate and gather information about it. I pulled Shubhankar and got off at the Theatre Road Bus stop.

We started to walk towards the Consulate; at least we thought we were going the correct direction but we were wrong. We asked someone about the direction of Consulate and reach there. Two policemen were guarding the Consulate and we asked them where the information desk was. We followed their instruction and came into a beautiful office. At reception desk there was a very beautiful girl who was made for that office only; at least I thought so. She gave a beautiful smile and asked – how can I help guys?

We were nervous, did not know what exactly to ask, our words were not coming out of the mouth. We nervously said a few words which sounded like "we go to America, no student, work, work and stay in America." We stared at one another; we were relieved that somehow we spoke to her.

The young lady at the counter probably heard this type of English million times. So it was not difficult for her to understand. She asked "do you want to immigrate to USA?"

We quickly replied –yes.

What is your educational qualification – she wanted to know.

We both replied – we passed B.Pharm from Jadavpur University.

Oh, you are in pharmacy. Yes, America needs pharmacists. Please wait, I am going to give you a form – she said smilingly. She got up from her chair and collected the forms and gave them to us and said – you can fill this form now and give back to me. She also told us that we could sit on that table and fill in the forms in her office.

We moved to the corner and started to fill in the forms. It took us about twenty minutes. After filling the forms we came back to the receptionist and told her – we have finished filling in the form.

She took our forms and told – we are going to give this form to our immigration department and they will contact you in next one month. Now you can go home and wait for our immigration department's letter. Good luck. Then she looked at someone else who was waiting for her attention.

Both of us came out of the office and looked at the watch. 3:30 in the afternoon that means our movie time is gone for that day. Subhankar said – what should we do now?

I said – let us have some tea and then may be; we can visit our friend Tulsi in his office. It is about ten minutes walk from here. We entered a coffee shop. The waiter showed us a table to sit. We settled in that table and asked for tea and some snacks.

Both of us were working in big firms. Big firm did not mean fat salary. I could get by with my salary. I have a family which was dependent on my income. So, immigration visa or no visa, I have to take my steps very carefully. My family's future is connected with me. For my friend, story is different. His family did not depend on his income. So, he had some freedom which I did not have. Freedom or no freedom, I was always ambitious and hard working. Once I decide to do something, I always started to act on it immediately. Waiting is not a game for me. I have learnt in life that acquiring certain things needs patience. In this situation patience is the name of the game. At that point I must have to wait for the response of the US immigration department.

Months passed by. I kept receiving one form after another. And I kept returning them to US immigration department. Finally, I received a letter for visa interview with the visa officer of US Consulate. I was waiting for it. I got nervous too because I had no idea what they would ask me or what they expect from me. Finally, interview date arrived and I also arrived to the US Consulate office for the interview. It was the similar scenario. One you woman was waiting for the candidates in the office. She was writing the names of the candidates and asking everyone to wait in the waiting area. We were waiting in the area. We hardly spoke to one another. If we did it was real low voice whispering to one another. About six or seven peoples were scheduled for interview on that day. As the day progressed they were calling the candidate for interview. I noticed one thing that the candidate was going in but not coming out. Later on I came to know that after the interview the candidates were asked to go out through a different path way. Finally my name was called around 11:30 am. I entered the interview room. It is a big room. An American Officer probably the visa officer was sitting in huge desk and there was another Indian girl who was helping him with paper works.

When I entered the room, the officer stood up and welcomed me and asked me to have a sit in front of his desk. I was nervous, started to sweat and looked for the handkerchief to rub my forehead to clean the sweat. The Officer looked at and asked – Dilip, why you want to go to America?

I replied – I want to go to America to have a better life for me and my family.

You have chosen New York City for you entrance to the country. Is there any reason? – He wanted to know. While he was talking to me he was also examining my papers.

I replied – New York City is the capital of business world, besides it is the melting pot of all ethnic groups; its charm is always glowing; I wanted to become a part of it.

After hearing my reply the visa officer extended his hand for a hand shake and said – congratulations! Please pick up your visa three days later. You have ninety days to travel to USA. Visa papers will be in an envelope and do not open it. You have to give it to immigration officer of New York JFK Airport. This seal must not be removed. If seal is broken, your visa will be cancelled. Now you can go and arrange for your travel to USA. Wish you all the best. Good bye.

I came out of his room. Stood for a while; felt a sigh of relief; finally I have received the visa for America. It was around noon time. Scorch rays of sun were cruel, I felt its cruelty; everything seemed to be red hot; I started to walk towards Esplanade. I received the visa; I still have to arrange money for the plane fare. Also I have to give a few thousand rupees for monthly expenses before I leave for USA. When I did not receive the visa, I did not have to worry about all these things. I decided not to worry about anything, let me share the good news with my family instead. I got on a bus which would take me to home, to family and to my father, the man despite being a widower has, done everything to give us a home filled with love and affection. So, I thought, he should be the first person to know about it and I should get his blessings before I start my journey for a new world. He is my father, friend philosopher, guide and my hero. I always tried to follow his footsteps. He is my unsung hero.

Three days later I went to American Consulate and collected envelope which contained the immigration visa. After I came out of the American Consulate, I looked at the envelope. This envelope is the passport to my new world, good or bad, my future filled with success or not; I have to win with my hard work and determination. All these thoughts started to come in my mind, an unknown fear and anxiety embraced my feelings. I wanted to control my emotions; fear of uncertain future was shredded its cover and give birth to hope and yearning in me. I came home from Esplanade. I was relaxed.

In the afternoon I sat next to my father with a cup of tea and some snacks. As usual, my father was smoking bidi and he asked me – how come you are home now? Didn't you go to work today? My father wanted to know why I was home instead of working.

No, I did not go to work today. I went to American

Consulate – was my reply. Then I started to bring the cat out of the bag little by little. I told him that I was going to America for a better future for me, for my family, brothers and sisters, for everybody. I also told him that I do not have any job lined up for me in America; I do not have any place where I can go for the first time. I also assured my father that thousands of peoples from all over the world were going to America and they all eventually find a job in their own profession. I won't be an exception either, I may not have the job now but when I go there I will definitely get one. Please do not worry about these; besides I have a few friends who are already there; some of them will definitely help me in settling down. Besides, they are my good friends, I helped them here on various occasions, I am sure, and they will try their best to help me out. I have full confidence in them.

After hearing me my father told me – I thought you were happy here. You have a reasonably good job, good salary and you work for good company. Do not count on the birds in the woods; count on birds what you have in your hand. You have seen me, after the partition, I had to move here; I lost everything in twenty four hours notice. We had a very good life, we were happy with it but in twenty four hours we lost everything; we pauper. So, think about it before you jump in the uncertainty of life. Besides, you are married now; did you consult your wife about this decision? Whatever you decide, I have full support for you. But make sure you consult your wife and then make the decision. I bless you son. Pray to God that your dreams come true. He embraced me; I knew; his blessings were showered on me. He also wanted to know how I was going to pay for the plane fare and all incidental expenses for the trip. I let him know in brief that I was going to withdraw the money from my provident fund and that money would be enough for my trip to America.

Same evening, I told my wife about the decision that I wanted to go to America. I also explained to her that I could not bring her with me because of the uncertain situation about the job and the place to live. She was worried to hear my plan and said – what happens if it did not work? Are you coming back? Whatever you earn here, we are happy with it. You should, I think, deliberate very carefully about this jump in the unknown dark sky for a better future. It is like an ocean. Nobody knows what is there under the waves in the deep sea. I told her – Muku, you are right; it is not easy, I am also worried to think that this decision will put us apart from one another. This separation will be very difficult for both of us. But trust me, like everything else we shall overcome the sadness caused by this. Our love for each other, our trust in each other will keep us together in spite of our geographic distance. Our love and respect for each other will always keep our hearts together. Our strong love will keep us connected all the times.

Thinking about the coming separation, her eyes started to glitter by the pearl drops which started to come down through her chicks. She could not control her emotions, she embraced me and said – Dilip, I am afraid, and I shall be all alone, I won't be able to stay without you. Please don't leave me alone here.

I understood her fear is reasonable and her worries are

reasonable as well. But I told her – everybody of our family loves you very much, especially my father will be here, nobody can put in harm's way in his presence. My family's love and affection will give you strength to sustain, you won't even remember me, soon you will think Dilip who. After that we joked around; we teased each other and then we promised to love each other and be together for the rest our lives. We hugged each other.

Next morning I went to my office and wrote my resignation letter. Until this point, it was easy for me to tell about my future plan. Now, I have to tell a person who has always helped me while I was studying in Jadavpur University. Without his help I would never be able to finish my education. He is the one who allowed me to work at night and study during the day. I can never thank him enough what he did for me. I shall always remain grateful to him. I went into his office. Always smiling man greeted me and asked me – everything ok. You are here early morning, what is the matter?

I was perplexed and did not know how to give the resignation letter. I was very nervous. I told him – sir, I want to resign from my job. I have received immigration visa in USA. I want to go there as soon as possible.

He replied – we have decided to promote you from next month. I was going to send you the appointment letter next week. Now, you are asking to resign. Do you know that USA has a very high rate of unemployment now? My suggestion; do not go, stay here, take the promotion and some day you will climb the ladder to the top. You are hard working and sincere; the company will treat you nice. I promise – you won't regret.

As long as I am here, I will take good care of you. He gave me all kind of assurance so that I do not quit. But I have made the decision. I could not reverse it.

I told him – sir, I apologize, I cannot stay. I shall always remember what you have done for me. If I do not succeed, please give me a job when I come back to India. He understood that no matter what I was not going to change my mind. He asked me – do you have place where you are going to live in New York.

No sir – I replied. I also mentioned that I am trying to find someone who would help me.

He said – my brother lives in America. He lives in Queens. He is here. Come to my home this evening, I will introduce you to him. May be, he can help you for it. In the meantime, think about your resignation and if you change your mind let me know.

Thank you, sir. I shall see you in the evening today. – I told him and left his office.

In the evening I went to my boss Mr. Mukherjee's house. Someone of his family asked me to sit in a couch of the living room. The room was very neatly decorated and I really like the way it was displaying a portrait of an elderly woman, probably his mother.

Oh, you are here. My boss entered the room while he was saying it me. I stood up and conveyed my respect to him, he asked me to sit down and said – I will be back. He left.

After a few minutes Mr. Mukherjee entered the room and another person followed him. Both of them sat on a couch in front of me. Then Mr. Mukherjee introduced his brother by saying – my brother Ramen, and this is Dilip works with me. Dilip has received an Immigration Visa for going to USA, he has no place to stay, I told him, may be, he can stay with you for a few days until he finds a place to live. And looked at Ramen and said – Ramen, what you think, can you help him?

Ramen looked at me and said – congratulations! Yes, you can come and stay with us until you get a job and find a place to go. Since both of us work, you have to do a few things on your own. Food will be in the fridge; you will have to take out and warm it and then eat it. Just try to become a family member and we will be there for you. I promise you got a place to stay in New York. Bye the bye when are you coming to New York?

I thank you very much. I am coming at the end of next month. I shall let you know exact date and time once I buy the plane ticket. – I told him. I thought in my mind – Ramen is a very nice person. He is my angel problem solver. I was overwhelmed by his kindness and generosity. He gave me his address and telephone number and told – please let me know the date and time; I shall be in the airport to take you to my home. Don't worry, your problem is solved. I am looking forward to receive you at the airport. He assured me of his help. The more I spoke to him the more I was convinced that he was one of the best persons I ever met. His humble attitude impressed me. After a few minutes I said good bye to him and promised that I would keep in touch with him about my journey. Thank God, a big load of uncertainty was off my shoulder. I came home relaxed.

Every night before going to bed my father and I always talked at least for half an hour. Should there be any good topic our discussion would even go beyond an hour. I was telling my father about Ramen and also told him that Ramen has agreed to host me in his place until I can arrange to be on myself. My father and I both opined highly about Ramen because it was always difficult to find a person who would be willing to help others. We thanked God for sending Ramen to us. It was late night. My father said – don't you have to go to work tomorrow? It is late, go to bed; see you in the morning.

Next few days went by in the speed of light. After my resignation accounting department of my office informed me that I was eligible to withdraw my provident fund and also I was eligible to get a gratuity for my services to the company. This news was a sigh of relief for me. This money would help me in buying my plane ticket and I would be able to leave some money for my family. That gave me a big hope that I would have done something for my family even though I would not be in home. I did not forget to speak to Ramen and gave him all the details about my flight and he told me not to worry; he would be in the gate to receive to me. I was assured that I would not have any problem whatsoever. I thanked him and we hanged the phone.

Finally the day came. All my family members came to see me off in Dum Dum Airport. My father hugged me and blessed me and said – always believe in yourself and never lose faith in God. God will keep eye on you. Never give up. Do not worry about us. We shall be fine. Write me a letter when you reach there. Every member of the family was in a happy mood, because one of them was going to America. I said - good bye. Then I proceeded towards the gate for departure. I should remind everyone that security check for getting into a plane was practically nonexistent in those days. Finally, I entered the plane and took my seat. My seat was next to window. Few minutes later a man sat next to me and introduced him to me. His name was Akhil Nath. I was looking downwards as the plane took off. Every object was becoming smaller and smaller as the plane started to go higher and higher. This was the first time for me to fly in a plane. I had a strange mixed feeling of sadness and happiness which I could not explain at that time. I felt like I jumped into the deepest see of uncertainty of my future; but deep down my heart I knew that I would find the pearl of my future someday. I was overwhelmed in the dream of future. At this time I heard Akhilda's voice – Dilip, where are you going, is someone coming to pick you up? He looked at me with a question in face.

I told him – Akhilda, yes, Ramen is coming to pick me up and I am going to live with him until I find a job. He lives in Brooklyn, so I am going to Brooklyn now with Ramen.

I am going to Forest Hills with my friend. He also assured me that I can live with him until I find a job. Akhilda told me.

Finally our journey ended in JFK. I came through the immigration and they gave me a card which is known as Green Card. Akhilda said – Dilip, bye, stay well and God willing we will see each other again. Then he stepped away with his friend who came to pick him up. I was looking around to see if Ramen had come but I did not see him. At this time, someone approached me and asked – are you Dilip?

I replied – yes and you.

I am Adhir Mukherjee, Bimal Mukherjee's brother – he replied. He also added – I have come here to pick up the shoe my brother sent with you. Where is the person who was supposed to pick you up? It is almost an hour since you are here, does he know that you were coming in this flight? He seemed concerned.

I told him worriedly that I spoke to Ramen and gave the flight number and the time of arrival to him and he promised he would come to take me home. I told Adhir.

Do you have his phone number with you? Let me give him a call – Adhir said.

Adhir made the phone call and gave the phone to me. Phone was ringing. Someone picked up and said – hello, may I know who is calling?

I said – may I talk to Ramen please.

She said – hold on please. I overheard she was saying – phone is for you.

The voice asked - who is it? His wife said – I don't know. Then she asked me – may I know your name?

I said – I am Dilip, just came from Calcutta, I am supposed to come to your place to for a few days.

She conveyed the message to Ramen. I heard that voice was telling her to tell me that he was not home. Then she told me – sorry, my husband Ramen is not home, he went to Philadelphia for an urgent reason. He cannot come to pick you up. She dropped the phone. I was at a loss what to say or what to do. Adhir asked me – what did he say? Is he coming to pick you up? I replied to Adhir – firstly she told me to hold the phone, spoke to someone and wanted to know my name. After that she spoke to that man and told me the Ramen was not home, he went to Philadelphia; they cannot take me to their home. Now, I do not know what I am going to do. I have only seven dollars with me. I was very frustrated and worried by this irresponsible behavior rendered by Ramen. I looked at Adhir and said – honestly, I do not know what I will do now.

Adhir understood that I was helpless at that point. He looked at my eyes and said – I am a student, live in a very small place, you come with me for now, then we will do some arrangement for you tomorrow. Do not worry; I shall give you eighty dollars for your five hundred rupees which you gave to my brother in Calcutta. Now let us take the subway for my place.

I was shocked by the lies Ramen told me. I remembered vividly every word of assurance he gave me in presence of his brother. I could not even imagine how a man can put someone in such a perilous and helpless situation. He knew, I only had seven dollars with me. Seven dollars meant nothing. Yet knowingly he put me in a detrimental situation. What happened to all those promises he made. I wondered if he had one drop of honest blood in his body. Ramen closed the door for me but Adhir came like an angel and opened another door for me. God is up there. Ramen proved himself to be the black sheep of the family. It took us about an hour to come to Adhir's place in Manhattan. Its name was Clinton Arms Hotel. Adhir had a small room with a common kitchen and bathroom. Adhir said – this is my room. Tomorrow I shall try to get a room for you here. Now go take shower and here is your eighty dollars which you gave to my brother.

I was tired and mentally destroyed by the action of Ramen. So, I took the towel and stepped towards the bathroom. I did not know that more surprise was waiting for me. When I was walking in the hall way, I saw Akhilda just came out of the bathroom. I thought he went to his friends place in Forest Hills. He was supposed to be there until he found a job. I asked – Akhilda, what happened?

It was embarrassing for Akhilda. He spoke very highly of his friend but his friend acted in a complete opposite way. Akhilda said – my friend cannot keep me with him so he dropped me at this place and left. In a way it is good; I do not have to take his favor.

I smiled and spoke – Akhilda another break of promise. What is your room number? Let me take shower and I will come to your room and talk. I went to the bathroom.

When I went back to Adhir's room, dinner was ready. Rice, dal, cabbage and buffalo carp. Food tasted very delicious. Adhir informed me that in the mean time he has found a room for me in this place. Rent was nine dollars every week. Next morning I could shift to my room. I was very tired physically and mentally. I needed rest and probably a sound sleep for a few hours. I told Adhir about Akhilda and told him – I thank you from the bottom of my heart for giving me a shelter and food. I shall always remain grateful to you for your kindness. I did not know what I would have done if he did not extend his helping hand to me. Ramen promised me to help and broke his promise and did not even care what might happen to me without his assistance; on the other hand you did not have to do it; yet you decided to help me; I cannot thank you enough. Please accept my gratitude.

Adhir smiled and said – you do not have to thank me, you do not have to express any gratitude either, I did what any human being should do; help another human being when they needed one. I just wanted to be a human being. Then said – I have a test on Monday, so let me study and you are tired, so you go to sleep. We shall talk tomorrow in the morning.

Next morning I shifted to my newly rented room. It was very small room with a bed and two windows. I opened the windows and immediately fresh spring breeze embraced me. I took a deep breath and smelt the air. Although my future was uncertain, I still had to find a job but I was thrilled that finally I sowed the seed of my life in America. In the same morning, I went to the store called "Key Food" and bought some utensils and some groceries for cooking. It was not easy to decide what to buy because that store carried the items hardly known to me and there were no Indian spices. So, I made it simple, I bought some rice, salt, potatoes and eggs; my shopping was done. For next few days my menu for lunch and dinner was boiled egg, boiled potato and rice mixed with butter. I always felt my cooking was delicious and I enjoyed every bite of it.

From next morning I started to find a job. On the third day of search I found a job in Duane Reade Drug store. Salary was $2.40 dollars per hour. That was my first employment in the country of opportunity. My dream train started to roll; for that moment I was the happiest guy on the face of the earth.

Days went by, months passed by, before I realized a year went by and financially I was ready to bring my wife, Muku from India. I rented a small one bed room apartment in Sunnyside, Queens. Rent was cheap, $140.00 dollars. I furnished the apartment with very cheap furniture. Yes, these comprised of a double bed, small dining table with four chairs and a television, believe it or not; it was a color television. In the mean time, I sent the plane ticket for my wife, one way fare was about $550.00 dollars. I did not have the money for fare; I borrowed from my friend Ranjan. He was very kind to help me out for it. I paid him back a few months later. I am grateful to him for his kindness. Later on he moved to Houston. After a few days I received a phone call from my father. He said that they have received the plane ticket. He also mentioned that Muku's flight number and time when she was coming to JFK airport. My father was relieved that his daughter-in-law was going to join his son in a few days. He also said – our daughter-in-law is a very nice person; you please take good care of her; never do anything which may make her morose or unhappy; remember one day she will be the pillar of your family. He also blessed me and said – son, someday you will be very fortunate, please try to share your good fortune among them who do not have it. Before I could say anything the line got disconnected. In those days telephone system was not as developed as these days. I was sad my conversation with dad ended so abruptly that I could not enjoy talking to my father. I was happy to know that my wife was going to join me in a few days in my Sunnyside apartment. The very idea became a reason for happiness. Many months loneliness was coming to an end soon. The very idea was joyful for me. Finally winter of loneliness was ending with the arrival of spring called Muku in my heart of seasons.

Finally the day came. It was a Saturday. I was so excited that I called the Air Lines and wanted to know if she was in the flight. The agent asked me to hold and then said – she is in the flight and her plane will arrive in JFK at about 4:00 pm. I thanked him. Bye the bye you could get this kind of information from the Air Lines in those days. 9/11 has changed the whole dynamic of daily life; we cannot get these small things anymore, thanks to the terrorist Islamic groups.

Finally her plane landed at JFK and I was waiting in the lobby of terminal four for her arrival. It took her about half an hour to go through the immigration process. Finally my waiting came to an end, I saw Muku was coming; she looked little nervous and she was looking all around probably to find me, I called her name and said – I am here. I walked to her and took her suite case from her hand. Then we started to walk towards the exit door to catch a cab. On our way to our home Muku was looking outside the cab and I could sense that she became astonished by the grandeur of the city and big buildings of the city. I felt world's biggest surprise in her eyes. I told her – enjoy the greatness of outer world of this country but please don't be discouraged by the humble appearance of our apartment. You will see how small an apartment can be. I smiled at her.

She said – does not matter how small it is, for two of us, I know, whatever we have would be enough for two of us. We were so absorbed in conversation that even before we realized our travel ended. We came home. I opened the door of the apartment and told her – this is your home. Now you sit and rest, I am going to make tea for you. I went to the kitchen. While I was making tea, I noticed, she was looking around the apartment and came to me and said –who arranged the furniture? This room looks nice. She admired my arrangement. I gave her the cup and said – now finish the tea and freshen up; if you want take shower. I showed her the bath room. I am going to make a phone call to let my father know that you arrived safely.

In the early evening we started our dinner. Menu was lentil, rice and egg curry. We sat down and she said – I am so lucky that you have made every arrangement for me so that I do not have any problem. I want to let you know that I am thankful and grateful for it. My first day in America is great; you made it great for me. From now on I will take care of the home. You just teach and help me know how to do them. We talked and talked. We talked about everyone of our family members. She was very emotional when she spoke about my father. I put my father's picture on a wall of living room. She stood in front of that picture and said – my father passed away when I was very young, I hardly remember him, your father gave me so much love and affection that I never felt that he is my father-in-law, I always thought that he is my father. By getting married to you I found my father. I will miss him a lot. It is good that he is here with us in our home. Frankly, I do not feel it is my first day in America; you made it so comfortable for me. How was your first day? Did Ramen come to pick you up in the airport? She looked at me for my reply.

I was thinking, should I tell the truth? But it was over. I did not have any bad feelings about that incident or about him. I did not know in what situation he had to decline me, who was I to judge him? I told her – no, he did not come to pick me up. Although he was home, he did not take me to his place; he did not give me any shelter. But God sent someone else for me; Adhir took me to his place. So, it was not that bad. Besides Adhir was a very nice human being. I am glad Ramen did not come. Because if he would have; I would not know Adhir. When you meet Adhir you will find out why I am saying it. I promised on that day that I shall always try to help them who do not have a place to go on the first day of their arrival; I shall offer them a shelter for first few days. I hope you will agree with me in this mission.

My wife was a very kind hearted person. She would take extra steps to help others. Knowing her I always believed she would strengthen my hands for other's cause.

I looked at the watch. It was late night. I told her you must be tired. You should go to sleep. I was sleepy too. I lied down and thought about the whole incident. What a contrast of value, in one hand Ramen, a betrayer, on the other hand Adhir, a pioneer and champion of humanity. Before I fell asleep, I promised, I would always try to help my fellow human beings when they need one. I also thanked my father for his advice to believe in God and I respectfully thanked God for saving me from a disastrous situation which might take place on the first day of my life in New York City. Eventually Adhir and me became good friends and never forget to mention that Adhir was my rescuer from a perilous situation.

She told me – get up and come with me. She held my hand and brought us in front of my father's picture and said - taking a lesson from your helpless situation let us promise to ourselves and we vowed in front of our father – if anyone known or unknown who was coming to USA needed a place to stay until they find a job, he would have got a place, my place for as long as he took to stand in his feet. Over the years, with our father's blessings and God's grace we have always been able to keep our promise.

(All the names are imaginary to preserve the privacy)

RELIGIOUS JUSTICE IN GREAT NATION OF INDIA

⁓

When India was divided in 1947, it was thought that Hindus will move to Hindustan (India) and Moslems will move to Pakistan. Unfortunately, that did not happen, majority of Moslems decided to stay in India and a significant number of Hindus migrated to India while a large number of Hindus decided not to leave their ancestral homes, and thought they would live with harmony and peace with their Moslem counterparts as it was before the partition. Soon the dream of living together with harmony and respect was shattered by the greed and injustices of Moslem counter parts. The real beast in Moslems started to come out and oppression of Hindus became a day of order, the East Pakistan Government became an accomplice for these atrocities and injustices against the Hindu population. Extortion, rape of Hindu girls or women and forceful conversion to Islam among Hindus became the order of the day. Hindus never got any help against these barbaric acts from the ruling government, police would not even take any complaint against any Moslem who committed these crimes on

Hindu population. And then the rise of the fundamental Islamic movements in Bangladesh started to destroy the Hindu temples at large, forcefully occupy the properties which belonged to the Hindu families. For example, any Moslem neighbor may ask to borrow some money from his Hindu neighbor, if he gives the money he will never return it to the lender and if he does not lend then he will face robbery and physical tortures on the same night; it is like a two way sword which tortures both ways. Consequently Hindu population in Bangladesh started to decline, some fled the country, and others were killed by the Moslems some others were being converted to Islam.

On the other hand the Moslems who decided to stay India they were receiving royal treatment from the Indian Government and politicians. In India same law never applied to the Hindus and Moslems, the family planning never applied to the Moslems; in some cases they received extra quotas for employment etc. all the corrupt politicians tried to buy Moslem votes by giving them extra benefits. Moslem community in India understood very well that their votes are necessary important tools for these corrupt politicians; they started to procure benefits out of these situations and also started to demean the Hinduism and specially in West Bengal and Assam Moslems started to infiltrate from Bangladesh in large numbers and by the help of corrupt politicians and government officials they obtained citizenship of India. As a result some of the districts in West Bengal became Hindu minority. In these districts the Moslems started to adopt Shariya law for themselves and also in some cases for Hindus also in those areas and Government usually looks in a different direction so that they do not have to take any action against those criminal activities. This way Government bureaucrats can please the corrupt politicians and return get rewarded in different ways by those same politicians. Any legal action taken against the miscreants of Moslem Community often tried to be portrayed as atrocities and injustices committed against the minority Moslem Community and nobody whether Government or Politician likes to be labeled the same. And as result of this denial of justice for the victims of wrong doings of the Moslem Community often never get the justice, and perpetrator never gets the punishment; subsequently perpetrators audacity and wrong doing keep growing more and more, often Hindus are their main prey. Another strange phenomenon that bothers me is that none these media, be it newspaper or television, never raise a hue and cry about these incidents, but when Hindus stand up against these atrocities and perpetrators are defeated, the media goes crazy and often depicts that Hindus are creating an atmosphere where Moslem cannot exist in peace in India anymore. Such bigotry and biased opinion of media often put the people of Hindu religion in an untrue turf of wrong doings against Moslems. It is very unfortunate to see that media has lost its primary responsibility of neutrality of any news related to conflicts between Hindu and Moslem. They never dig into the truth and never depict the truth with neutral mind, instead they always opt for the Moslem brothers. So, media should be held responsible for the dominance which the Moslem Community often enjoys in India. Indian Constitution does not treat Hindu and Moslem religion equally, often Moslem religion is treated with special affection where they get away with many social issues like marriage, employment etc. they are often given extra privilege where peoples of Hindu religion never allowed to enjoy those benefits. Now time has come that the Constitution treats the citizens of India equally with same importance otherwise India will be converted to an Islamic Country in fifty years. In the meantime, Islam has taken another cunning path to convert Hindus into Moslems. In West Bengal, Moslem children are given Hindu names like Amal, Beena etc. and if you ask their name they will respond by saying 'Amal, Beena' etc. and never mention the last name. These children eventually go to college and fall in love with their Hindu counterpart and the Hindu counterpart never knew the true identity of Moslem boy or girl because they only tell you their first name. When the question of marriage comes then the true identity of the Moslem boy or girl comes out and then the Moslem boy or girl demands that Hindu boy or girl must convert into Islam otherwise marriage will not take place. Most of the time the Hindu boy or girl succumb to the situation and convert himself or herself into Islam, eventually another Hindu is converted, another Moslem added to their community. Apparently it looks like one or two incidents but if you add them in them, collectively it becomes a big number every year. If Hindu social leaders fail to realize the consequence of this social issue then eventually Hindus will lose the ground of majority in India in fifty or so years. Now it is up to the Hindus if they want to keep their country or give it up to turn it into an Islamic state. The country that was established for the people of Hindu religion is now on the verge of diminishing for the inaction or no action of the Hindus and the Government as well. What will happen, it is in hands of future generation, but if we fail to recognize this threat then we failed our next generation to present them a secure country, a secure society in which they will grow with freedom and love for others and love for the humanity in general in my country and great nation of India.

RETIREMENT –
A ROCKING JOYFULNESS

~

God has created the human beings in his own way. Every living animal in this world has a meaning for its own existence. Some live for others, some live of others, some even tries to destroy others for their own interest. But human race is the most powerful living object who can think, who can determine their own fate by their own activities. Unlike other living species human beings are equipped with some rare elements which are normally not found in any other animal. Although some of them are very intelligent in nature, however they are not very much prone to judgement for their action. Mostly they work by the influence of their own instinct for survival. But the Homo sapiens are different, they have mind, they have judgement, they have ability to think and determine what they want to have next in life. The most unique creation of nature and God is the human being. Among all the animals the human being is the most important who possesses all the qualities of being superior in every respect to other living creatures. Since times immemorial human race has taken the civilization in their hands and created today's world of Science, literature and technology. This evolution did not take place in one day, one month or one year, it was created by many ages of periods like ice ages' era to modern era, they have created things of their needs, they have invented to follow their dreams, took a few hundred years and an industrial revolution to make this world of this success of technological and other developments for physical and mental pleasure. Life of a human being can be divided in four general stages namely childhood, adulthood, mature family life, retired life and finally of renunciation. This has been described very uniquely and effectively in Hinduism. In Hinduism from birth to end of life has been divided in four stages. These stages are described as "Chaturashramas" in Hiduism for many thousands of years.

The four ashramas are: Brahmacharya (student), Grihastha (householder), Vanaprastha (retired) and Sannyasa (renunciate). The Ashrama system is one facet of the Dharma concept in Hinduism and Hindus have always shown great belief and respect for this "Chaturashramas". Among all the animals, only human being has the luxury of having "Vanaprastha" retirement. In other animal world, if they do not work or prey, they die of starvation, but for human it is different, they can stop working and still can live a decent life with the savings of working life and enjoy the life to the fullest extent with his family and friends by planning effectively for future years according to his desire how he wants to spend the rest of his life, This is possible only for human beings because only human beings know how to save for the future days or years, no other animal has this perception or ability to do this.

Firstly a prospective retiree must get rid of all debts. Secondly in my opinion, retirement for anyone needs an adroit and effective planning. Firstly a prospective retiree must get rid of all debts. Usually retirement has two segments of planning, one is financial and the other one is socially wellbeing. Financial planning can be done with a financial planner according to someone's living standard, an income goal can be set from the accumulated wealth by investing the finance in an efficient way with the help of the financial planner. Most of the time the retiree's home is free and clear of any mortgage and that way a big chunk of money is saved and this can be used for other expenses. From my experience I have found that unplanned hidden expenses are more frequent and more expensive. I can give you a few examples which I did not foresee or anticipate before my planning but it is also true that good or bad I have never lived a budgeted life, so I did not anticipate or realize that under-planning could bring a limitation to someone's living standard or habit. I shall try to give a few examples which I have experienced in my early retired days. Since you don't have to join the rat race any more you may decide to have lunch two three days a week. Occasionally your friends will join you and you would love to treat them, you may have visited more Puja Mandaps than you were visiting before and it costs for subscriptions, you go to watch grandchild's game and he or she wants to go to lunch or dinner with you after the game, another one

I find really difficult to sustain when someone indulges in unnecessary habitual shopping, that can put anyone in large debt if they use the credit card regularly. Sometimes people become shopaholic which can eventually destroy the family harmony and peace. Two evils, alcoholism and gambling are commonly seen among non-Indian retirees, however, some of my Indian Retiree friends are already became victims of these and some of them are seeking professional help and trying to come out of this kind of addiction, Traveling is another example. Since you have enough time in hand you may start more traveling and it will soon put you in expenses. So, if you exercise constrain to your new found liberty in a moderate way, you should be able to steer your freedom to your advantage.

After retirement some of the retirees move to some fifty plus community. These communities are good but remember they have some sort of restrictions where your children or grandchildren may not be allowed to live for a long time. Normally in these communities, children are not allowed to live continuously, so your grandchildren may not find any playmates. Please look into these matters before you make a move for these communities.

Since a retiree does not work daily, he has about ten to twelve hours in hand every day and some of them do not know how to manage that time on a daily basis. The other problem usually shows up because of poor social mingling and communication skills. Indians, in general, like to mingle with their fellow Indians, this inherently create a potential problem because when someone retires all his friends are usually working, so he cannot mingle with his friends except weekends. So time management is an important issue for any retiree but do not panic, there is a whole new world where you can spend your time very joyfully.

Retired, congratulations, a new world is waiting for you, where you can enjoy rest of your life very happily. Time hangs heavy, don't worry, there are so many ways to use the time that you will soon find out that you do not have time for this for that etc. Nobody likes to live an idle life. Almost every town in USA has a "Senior Citizen Center". These are very unique and versatile institutions. They support the retirees and seniors very effectively. Join your local Senior Center and they will help you to grow new interest in anything you like. Usually they have different groups for Music, Literature. Poetry, Painting, Cooking Sports, Yoga etc. You can join any one of these groups and learn your new interest skillfully and enjoyably. Also Recreation department of any town sometimes teaches how to play games like Tennis, Golf etc. Anyone who likes sports can learn these and make many new friends of his choice.

USTA (United States Tennis Association) has its branch in every County. Regularly they promote tennis and anyone can join USTA and join the learning sessions. It is a wonderful sport which help to get all kind of exercises, like running, stretching, strengthening muscles, toning muscles, eye hand coordination and many more, tennis gives a very effective Cardio, tennis players do not need go to the Gym, it is a whole platter of exercise. Another beauty of this game is that age is not a factor for this game, I have seen peoples in their nineties are playing this game. I have seen these tennis players come from all walks of life. Personally I am a member of a group like this. In our group we have about twelve players and all of them are professionals like lawyers, teachers, doctors, financial advisors etc. When you become friends with them, experienced advice is free for you. Once I was in a situation where I needed some legal advice my tennis friend not only gave the advice he fought the case on my behalf and did not charge a dime until the case was over. This might be an extreme situation but friendly advice is always available from friends like them. When I moved to my present residence all my tennis friends wished me good luck and expressed that they would always miss me, for me this was an overwhelming experience and I shall always miss my tennis buddies, like Nina, Elaine, John and all others. Tennis friendship becomes like a family friendship. Every year Nina gives a luncheon party in her Hudson viewing Apartment for our group and I shall miss the party and my tennis friends from the bottom of my heart until last days of my life...

Most effective planning for retirement is good but it is not immune to new problems. Retiree may find an obstacle which he never anticipated. To tackle this type of situation I personally follow my rule of I.A.A. (Identify, Address and accept). It is very simple, identify the problem, address the problem and then accept the solution.

Every retiree has worked hard for the past several years for this day of life when he does not have to join the rat race every morning of his life. You worked hard, now is the time to rip the benefits of it. Retirement is worth living, worth enjoying and worth sharing with your friends and families with newly found life style. If someone plans right his retired life will rock and he will give slogan "rock retiree rock."

SEVADASI

—

This village is near a big city in Andhra Pradesh also it is miles away from one of the biggest temples in Andhra Pradesh. Andhra Pradesh is also known for the temple of Tirumala Venkateswara, an ornate hilltop shrine to Hindu's Vishnu in the southern part of the state, it is visited by millions of Hindus every year. This village has a tradition going thousands of years of having different temples of different Hindu deities and the villagers always showed their respect to these Gods and Goddesses. Some of the families lived here for hundreds of years and they maintained the old tradition, be it religious or social or simply here say, every old value has a special meaning to these villagers. Life here is pretty much religious which is controlled by the Brahmins and Priests of these temples. Padma's family is living in this village for many years, her family is one of the oldest families in the village. For generations her family worked for the local temple. The priest of the temple always treated her father with love and respect. Her father donated many acres of land to the local Vishnu's Temple and this temple used to get a substantial income from the land which was donated by Padma's father. Since her father's passing away she took over the family business and continued to follow her father's footsteps. But lately, she is facing a problem from one of the Devdasi named Lakshmi of their temple. This Devdasi Lakshmi is a middle aged very beautiful woman who was married to Deity by the Priest of the temple. During her young days most of the village men came to her and she satisfied them with her young and luscious body. Devdasi Lakshmi believed that when she whets the sexual appetite of any man, she is serving her God to whom she was married to. Whenever she consummated physical relation with any man it was a worship to her for her God to whom she was married to. This was her belief, she was trained to believe this dogma. Those days it was very normal that a man would make an appointment with Devadasi and come to her, after fulfilling his urge he would have pay her too. A Devdasi would live on by begging alms, they would go from house to house and beg for alms. Most of the households would donate food or vegetables to any Devadasi, although the women of these households knew that probably her husband or young son had sex with her. It was an acceptable fact to all the married women, to all the families and to any locality including most part of the country. And for the Devadasi, it was a matter of pride that they were providing an important service to the community and there by serving the God. This belief was deeply inculcated in the minds of these Devadasis. Consequently they all believed that any female child born out of their womb must opt for becoming a Devdasi to maintain the tradition and glory of the life of a Devdasi. Devdasi Lakshmi also believed this and she also wanted to see her young daughter's life was also dedicated to the cause of the God in their temple. So, one day she went to see the head priest of the temple who performed the rituals when she was made a Devdasi, she bowed and touched his feet to do Panama and said – Lord, my daughter's "Ritu Kala Samskara Ceremony" is coming soon". It is also known as "Ritushuddhi" ceremony when a girl wears sari for the first time. It is the celebration when a girl's rite of passage after menarche (first menstruation) and she is reckoned as a young woman both physically and spiritually as well. This ceremony is considered to be the right time for a girl to dedicate her life to the God and be declared a "Devdasi". From this point she belongs to the temple and she is trained to learn the art of dance and music to perform in front of God and an assembly of crowd in temple. Similarly they are also trained mentally and spiritually to believe that they are really born to augment this tradition of serving the God. She truly believed it and she wanted that her daughter, Suvadra, also embraces the life of a Debadasi.

She also said - I want that she also follow the life of Devdasi and continue the tradition of my family. Lakshmi also added "you are a pious man, in fact I consider you my God, and as such I beg you to become her first God for the services as I was privileged to do the first service of my life to you. Please let her have this privilege when she marries the Deity and enters the life of a Devadasi for the first time."

Priest listened carefully to Lakshmi. It is very common that head priest becomes the receiver of first service given by these newly dedicated girls. Over many years he has received it, it is a mundane pleasure which turns divine for him, and he has no reason to refuse it. He said "before I agree with your proposal, I want to speak to your daughter, Suvadra. Bring her to me one day, I shall see if she is mentally ready and pious enough for the sacrifice of becoming a Devadasi."

Lakshmi said respectfully to the priest – yes my Lord, I shall bring her to you as soon as possible. Then she left the temple for her house.

In the evening Lakshmi and her daughter Suvadra were having dinner after praying to the God in their home. Lakshmi knew that Suvadra was very much tired physically because she was playing with her friends, some of them are children of Devadasis like her. Suvadra never understood the idea and philosophy of being a Sevadasi, why her mother has to go from house to house for alms, why her mother could not work and make a living like any other person in their village. It was very painful for her to see that her mother would "sit" with three four men every day in the name of serving God. She never liked it and she decided that she will go to school and educate herself and eventually get a job to live a normal life like any other person of their neighborhood. The teacher of the local school liked Suvadra very much because she was very brilliant in studies. He used to advise –Suvadra, do not leave the school and become a Devadasi like your mother. Instead stay in school, go to college and educate yourself, there is a bigger world waiting for you. His inspiration really ignited the fire of yearning of becoming someone in her life and she decided to go any length to achieve her goal. Even in her early days she was very wise in her thoughts and she realized only person who can help her stay in school is Padma Akkaya who supports the temple with her wealth. Everyone in the area revered her and would abide by her decisions. So, Suvadra decided to see her and beg her help for pursuing the dream of her life to get a good education.

One day Suvadra went to Padma's home and met her. Padma gave a real good attention to what Suvadra said. Padma already knew about the intention that Suvadra's mother wants her to marry the deity of the temple and become a Devadasi. Padma was impressed with this little girl's idea of life and said – Suvadra, if you get a chance, after finishing your studies, what you want to do with your life?

Suvadra said –Padma Akkaya, after I finish my education, I want to become a Sevadasi for these Devadasis so that these Devadasi will never have to "sit" with any man and never have to act like a prostitute in the name of serving the God. I want to abolish this "Devadasi Pratha" from the society and make a better place in the society so that nobody ever is dedicated to deity for becoming a Devadasi who satisfies the sexual appetite of man in pretense of serving the God. I want to help these Devadasis to rehabilitate them to a life of dignity and honor where they could decide for themselves about their lives. I want to serve these Devadasis in their needs and become their Sevadasi so that a Devadasis gets the respect back in this decadent society where she could choose her own destiny and live happily ever.

Note - "The law was passed in the Madras Presidency and gave **devadasis** the legal right to marry and made it illegal to dedicate

girls to Hindu temples. The bill that became this act was the
Devadasi Abolition Bill. Periyar E. V.

Bill: Devadasi Abolition Bill
Enacted by: <u>Madras Presidency</u>
Enacted: 9 October 1947"

SEXUAL YET POLITICAL ASSAULT

———

In the wake of rampant sexual harassment, assault and rape charges against many celebrities and congressmen, much has been said and practically nothing has been done to deter this kind of behavior towards women. Now from these events, if we analyze carefully it is evidently clear that allegations in congress and senate are treated differently than those of private sectors.

In recent months so many allegations came out against the powerful celebrities that it is clear that these perpetrators are like animals who have no regard for human life or women in general. These inhumane behaviors did not happen in one or two months, rather these attacks were planned deliberately and executed ruthlessly for many months and in some cases for many years and the victims of these attacks were very afraid that they could be harmed physically or financially by removing them from their employments. Despite being humiliated for so many months or years they could not find strength or courage to bring these assaults due to fear of character assassination and stigma of bad names.

The most infamous incident in recent history of sexual abuse and assault was done by none but our Ex-President Bill Clinton in the oval office of White House with a very young intern Monica Lewinsky. At first, he denied the allegations by giving a speech to the nation and completely denying that she had any sexual relation with white house intern Monica Lewinsky. Bill **Clinton** has faced multiple allegations of **sexual assault** and harassment, while consensual in some cases and sense, was nonetheless textbook sexual harassment of a subordinate of a kind that would get many CEOs fired or may even be tried in the court of law. Unfortunately, Bill Clinton's wife who claims to be the champion of woman's cause has vigorously opposed those women's accusations and also subsequently denounced those assaulted women. Democratic Party and it's Alliance liberal media put those victims in such ignominy that some of them went hiding so that they are not physically harmed. Media vigorously vilified those women, assassinated their characters and they also tried to trivialize sexual mayheim under the pretense that most of the high-powered men always keep a woman on the side other than his wife, it is not a big deal.

If we analyze the behavior, prowess of men in private sector and in gubernatorial arena belongs to the CEOs. Media Laurels, Movie Industry, Congress and Senate. They have money, position. Power and fame. These personalities should have used their strength and leadership to publicize that sexual impropriety towards women or child is not acceptable behavior in the society and it will not be tolerated, perpetrators will be prosecuted to the fullest extent of law, eventually they will get exemplary severe punishment for their inexcusable conduct.

Instead we see persons like Harvey Weinstein, Charlie Rose, Matt Lauer, Bill O'Reily, Congressman John Conyers, Senator Al Franken and others are engaged in so many cases of sexual impropriety, it seems that it is an epidemic where sexual predators prey on women for years together and never stand trial for their inappropriate behavior towards women. On the other hand, we find that these entities always try to hide these incidents and try to tarnish the characters the women who come forward to complain about these powerful men and establishments. It is evidently clear from the case of Matt Lauer. At first NBC CEO claimed this is the first time that they have received this complaint against M Matt Lauer, however under greater scrutiny it was very clear that Matt Lauer was engaged in these activities and it was an open secret in the NBC network. Even Katie Couric disclosed that Matt Lauer used to pinch her in the back frequently, however it was not clear from her statement whether she complained to the authorities of NBC. We also find that these men use their power to intimidate the women who work for them, quench their predatory sexual appetite and frighten them that they can lose their employment. If we look in the cases of sexual assault cases where perpetrators are members of Congress or Senate, they send the case to the Ethics Committee of the relevant house, we can also easily, easily find that there is always an endeavor to hide evidences under the rug or delay the process of investigation where the predators get plenty of time to manipulate so that the accused member gets a rubber stamp of innocence from the Ethics Committee. Unfortunately, now a days Senate and Congress has turned into a cesspool of corruption, they have lost the integrity and honesty. When they contest in election, they promise that they will do whatever is good for the citizens, they promise to uphold the interest of the country first, they will protect the constitution of the country and they will always protect the country from the enemies of outside or enemies within with deepest love for the country, but once they get elected, they forget the promise they made and start to work to fulfill his own interest only. They sell their honesty and integrity to the lobbyists and avarice wins their heart and mind and starts to fill their pockets, to win the next election, they start to accumulate their own treasure, often they forget that they made a promise to work for the citizens of the country. Ignoring the duty for which they have been entrusted with, they become a toy in the hands of lobbyists. We, the citizens of the country should demand that lobbying system should be abolished from both Congress and Senate. To cleanse the cesspool of corruption in both houses Senate and Congress should pass laws for limiting the terms for Congress for 6 yeas and that of Senate should be for two terms only. And none of the members of Congress and Senate or their relatives should never be allowed to lobby anymore. This way we can eliminate an authorized bribing system once and for all.

I also want to entreat these women who have been abused and mistreated should also think that their allegations may end so many careers untimely and they may even face judicial prosecution, for this reason alone they should not hide these incidents and get the benefits from the accused. It is also evidently clear from the accuser and accused that both are equally responsible for such act, one takes the advantage of situation and the other takes the benefits from the accused and keeps the mouth shut for many years and comes out when it is beneficial to her. Instead of hiding the facts of wrong doing, please come forward immediately to public and seek justice from the court of law, do not be ridiculous by coming out someone after twenty, thirty or even forty years, it only expresses that you are selfish, mean and think about yourself only, nobody else other than yourself only. Ladies, think about this fact that you have put this country through so much pain, agony, hatred and overall shame that this country is on the verge of moral division consequently dividing the country into two ominous division in the entire population in our great America.

In 2016 the people of USA has elected a Republican Party man as the President of United States, who is not an insider of Capitol Hill, who has no political experience whatsoever, this man speaks his mind, wants to make America great again, wants to make America free of all illegal immigrants, wants to establish the most powerful military might in the world again, he is none other than our President Donald J Trump, a very successful businessman and a real estate developer whose dynasty shines all over the world, but our Liberal and Democratic Politicians and supporters including media giants of television and newspaper cannot swallow the defeat of their sure candidate Mrs. Hillary Rodham Clinton. On the other hand, the seasoned Republican Party members of Congress and Senate also are very reluctant to accept him as the President. So, in every step of the way they are either delaying or creating hurdles so that President Donald J Trump cannot deliver his campaign promises, consequently his presidency suffers a severe historical failure in the history of United States Presidency. In this effort Liberals, Democrats and Republicans created a united "stalemate" in the government. Both sides of the political isle should realize that these old accusations are only delaying the process of progress of President Trump's agenda for our beloved country. Please stop these nonsenses and go back to work for the betterment of the country. Let our country's middle class expand and shine in glory again.

Ladies, due to your untimely exposure of accusations, we, the honest and hardworking citizens are hurting, the country is facing a shameful status in the entire world, your untimely allegations have caused serious injury to our country's sky-high reputation and injury and as a result our motherland is profoundly bleeding and probably it will leave a permanent scar in the face of our greatest nation on the face of the earth. Please let us work together so that we can recover and regain the fame and reputation of democracy and nation as a whole, our country will shine again in the sky of power and democracy in the world.

THE ATONEMENT

—

B imal Roy is a very familiar name in this small town. Town is called Ramgarh, it is about thirty miles from the main city of Ram Nagar, the state capital. In this state anything special has a name beginning with God's name. People of this city are very religious, be they are be of Islamic religion or be a Hindu, they always try to live their life according to their own choice or belief. Bimal Roy came to this town as a child with his father who took an employment as a teacher in the local high school. His father Amal Roy being displaced by the partition of India had nothing but his education and an exemplary skill to teach students to achieve their learning goals. Ram Nagar high school was very happy to get an efficient teacher like him. High School's Secretary Kamla Prasad was very happy to have a teacher like him. So, he started to speak to the School Managing Committee so that he could give a small piece of land where this able teacher could build a house for his family. Kamla Prasad was a lawyer and was very supportive of the school and its teachers and students as well. He was a pioneer educator and always wanted that children get the proper chance to educate themselves. On later days when one student from this school stood first in the final examination and this result was attributed to Amal Roy for his hard work, coaching and the guidance to the same student, the name of the school and the teacher were all over the state, many other schools started to offer employment for a higher position, better salary and compensation. But Amal Roy ignored all their offers and once said to the Secretary Kamla Prasad – Kamlajee, perhaps you have heard that many schools are offering me position of Head Master, but I have decided to not to leave this school because you have been so kind to me and my family that I cannot even think of leaving this school. If you allow me I shall teach in this school until my retirement. This school and this Ram Nagar have special place in my heart, I want to spend rest of life in here raising my family and be with my friends. Please help me in doing my job.

Kamla Prasad said in his response to Amal Roy – Masterji, we are very lucky to get a teacher like you, we feel even luckier to see that you have made your decision for staying here. I promise the school will pay due respect to you when the time comes. In the mean time I have a request, please keep this conversation between you and I because if other members know about it now they may have some pernicious thought about the present Head Master. You and both know and understand that our Head Master is also very good teacher and administrator. School needs his expertise also for now.

Amal Roy replied – Kamlajee, I understand it very well, besides I want to let know that my decision to stay here has nothing to do with the money or position, it is rather for the reason that we love this place and peoples of this place, we want to become part of this community and live here forever. After being displaced from our own land and house, this place has offered us peace and happiness for our family, this place and our neighbors have helped us to forget the agony of losing every mundane possession and our friends and neighbors have given us solace when our family and we needed it most, by leaning towards more money or higher position would be tantamount to betrayal to my own friends and family and I shall never stoop so low for my own benefit. We are happy here and we shall spend rest of our lives here in Ram Nagar. Besides, Kamlaji where am I going to get a friend and a well-wisher like you in the whole state, and you know my wife likes you as her brother, where is she going to get her brother to put Rakhi around his wrist, where is my son Bimal going to get his uncle Kamla and auntie Kusum in some strange place? God brought me here and we are going to live rest of our live here, no more moving anymore.

Years passed by, family is good, but problem showed up when Bimal passed the final examination of school, he declined to continue his education further, instead he wanted to work and make money. Bimal's parent were not happy with his decision of not going to college. Bimal's mother said – Bimal, you are a good student, finish college otherwise you will never get a good paying job. Besides, if you do not go to college, then what you want to do with your life? Please listen to us, go to college, finish the education then go for a good job. Son, don't be obstinate, listen to your mom and at least finish undergraduate level of college, your father is a famous teacher, being his son if you do not finish college, people show you and tell, look at him father is so highly educated and son did not finish the college, what a deplorable situation, please go to college at least for your father's sake, please.

Bimal listened to his mom very patiently. His father was by his side when his mom was pleading him for joining a college. His father did not say a word, all he did is listen to his wife's plea. Bimal has been a good kid all his life. He was good in school and after school activities. He was equally if not more dedicated to pro and extracurricular activities, in fact, he made his parents proud of him by dint of these qualities, like kindness, respect and feeling for others. During these years of his life he developed a unique interest for business and debated within himself to the fact that what he wanted to do with his life in his adult years. He went back and forth with this deliberation very carefully and only found the embedded yearning for business in his heart and soul. He reasoned that if he is going for business then he should start his journey now not after another few years of college. His resolve made him more determined to follow the path which he believed to be his fate in coming years. He looked at his mom and dad and said – mom and dad, all my life I have done whatever you asked me to do. I always dreamt to make both of you proud of me, I studied hard and did good in school, I worked hard to achieve my goals and you always supported me, often the results were up to your satisfaction, I am grateful that you always believed in me and my abilities. I want you to keep faith in me again and I promise I shall never fail you, on the other hand few years later you will be very happy that you let me follow the ambition of my life. As for the education, I promise, I shall pursue it to your satisfaction but I shall do it as an external student, I shall study every day and I shall take help from you dad. If you cannot for any reason whatsoever I shall find a tutor who will help me and I shall pay him from my business income. Please help me in pursuing my career.

They both heard him very clearly and felt that Bimal is very much set out to fulfill his dream with or without their approval and he does not get their approval, it may hurt him emotionally eventually may be psychologically which may preclude him from having a normal life, it is too big a risk for any parents to take, they must have to find a middle ground where family harmony will not be jeopardized. His dad made up his mind and said – Bimal, you are our only child, we want your happiness, we also want that any of your decision now precludes you from having a better life with good finance, as you know I am a school teacher, I shall never be able to leave any money for you. Since you are so confident about your decision, we shall support you with our whole heart and we bless you succeed in your life and consummate your ambition.

Then looked at his wife and said – higher education is not for everyone, some people may have some other talent and they should follow their instinct and talent, may be they have some other talent which will bring them success in every aspect of life, I am sure, our son will be a success in pursuit of his dream. Now let us pray for him. Whatever happens, God willing happens for the best.

Time flows like a river, never stops, it happened in this family also, days went by, months went by, years passed and the life of Bimal and his business dreams became brighter and brighter. Before anyone realized Bimal became a business magnet in the small town, everyone respects him for his philanthropic activities. He established a high school for girls in his parents' name, he established a college and a charitable hospital in his grand parents' name in the town. In fact his benevolent activities were showering the whole town whenever it is necessary, his treasury is open for all. When his parents asked him to get married and settle in life, he said – mom and dad, I only have one condition, I want to marry a widow of your choice, I hope you two will support me, I want to follow the ideals of Vidyasagar, I want to bring about a change in the society where young men will be motivated to marry widows. You find out the girl and let me know I shall marry her, I do not even want to see her before marriage, and your choice will be final for me. I know you will find the right girl for me, mom and dad, now get to work for me please, find your daughter-in-law.

Although it was a very unusual request from their son, parents of Bimal became very proud to see his resolve for changing the society to bring about a revolutionary change in the minds of young peoples to marry widows of the society. This is a many ages old prejudice against the women who lose their husbands for one reason or another, these women were becoming victims of the societal ill and prejudice. His mother said – Bimal, I am very proud of you. I am also delighted to see that you think about others and you are willing to sacrifice for the benefit of others especially the widows. Your father and I will find out a girl of your choice, and we shall find our daughter-in-law according to your desire.

Being imbued by Bimal his parents found a dream girl for their son. This girl was married at the age of twenty and lost her husband in a fatal car accident and since then she was living with her father-in-law, finished education with MA in English and was employed as a teacher in a local high school. Her in-laws treated her like their own daughter and they wished that she gets married again and spends her life with her new husband. Although her parents wanted her to go back to them but Aruna always declined to do so because she felt it her responsibility to look after them since they have lost their only son. Her idea was if she leaves this house then they would have nothing to cling on, she made them her own parents and this house her own. At first she was very reluctant to the idea of marriage, continuous persuasion coerced her to accept the proposal. Many years have gone by since they got married. Eventually they were blessed with three children, two boys and a girl. Now they are grown up and married. Two boys work in their father's business and the girl has been married to a doctor who lives abroad. They come to visit once every two three years. Bimal's family was going this way, every member of the family was happy but the rhythm went broke when Bimal's wife Aruna became bed ridden with an incurable ailment, his wife was center point of his family, for that Bimal was always very concerned about his wife's health. She became very frail, her eyes looked like went into chasm, she could not stand up, was so frail could not even sit down, had to lie down all the time, Bimal could see that his wife is shrinking on a daily basis, it is difficult to see the difference between her and the bed, looks like she is the part of the bed, like a long thin and flat roti (bread). She was suffering from very deep bedsores, her voice almost went away, she lost her appetite, she did not have urge to live anymore, practically she was longing for the final moment, the ultimate passing namely death. She always urged her husband – please do something so that I can go, I don't want to suffer anymore, please call a priest, I want to speak to him. It was really very hard for Bimal to see his wife's misery, he started to think and finally decided to speak to a priest for his wife's emancipation from this dire health situation. So, he went to the most learned Priest who was revered by all Pundits and explained the situation of his wife and asked – is there any Puja (worshipping) which can relieve my wife from this agony of pain? I cannot see her suffering this way. Please do something for her, all her life she did good for others, but now she is immersed in the sea of pain and sufferance. A good person like her should never be ion this situation. Finishing his beseeching to the Priest, Bimal looked at the priest, his face was pale, his eyes were watery, and he looked very helpless.

The priest listened to Bimal very carefully. Then he said – Bimal, nobody can stop the destiny. It is in God's hand, however we can try to alleviate her condition by doing some special oblation named "Shanti Swastayan" (propitiatory ablation) to remove the influence of evil spirits. It is a very hard to perform and it is better if her son does it. Do you think that your son will perform it for his mother's wellbeing? If he is willing to do it we may be able to satiate her fragile condition.

Bimal listened to the Priest and said – I have to ask my sons about it. Can a daughter perform this ritual? In case they decline to do it, can I perform this Puja? Now a days children are different, they think about themselves and their family only. They are not concerned about their parents like Bimal's generation.

The Priest listened to Bimal and replied – the result is expected if the eldest son performs it. Daughters are not allowed because after marriage they belong to different family origin. If sons decline, then husband can do it but that is not desirable. He also said – go home and ask your children, may be they will do it for their mother. Then he reminded that whoever does this ritual will automatically will be responsible for any sin committed by their mother. Please remember it.

Bimal came home worried how he is going to tell his sons for this Puja for elimination of their mother's sufferings. Bimal came home and called their sons to see him at home. Usually his two sons come home once a week, normally on Monday evenings. Their wives do not come on regular basis, they come whenever they want to see their in-laws, this is going on for many years, when his daughter comes from abroad, this arrangement changes, to accommodate the sister-in-law the brothers and their come to visit the house more because Bimal's daughter always stays with her father. After the children got married, Bimal and his wife help the children to establish their homes in separate houses and since then they live separately in different houses but always attend any family occasion and gathering with the family, in a way family is separated yet together when needed. This was Aruna's idea to keep and maintain family peace and harmony. Bimal came home and told Aruna about the atonement suggested by the Priest. Aruna heard about it but could not say anything because she was too weak to speak. She had a vacant look in her eyes. Looking at his wife Bimal felt helpless and remembered how his wife was always very talkative and brought happiness to his own parents and others by her kindness and supportive behavior to others who needed it most. He decided to call his two sons with their wives to come to his home next evening to discuss this worship of atonement to save his wife from her bad condition of health.

Bimal explained the idea of atonement to his sons and their wives and requested their sons – will you perform this ritual for your mother's health? According to the Priest the best result is obtained if the eldest son performs it, now if you agree, I want to finish it by next week, and if you do not want to do it then I shall perform it for your mother's sake.

Both of his sons asked – daddy, do you really believe in this ritual? This is nothing but some bad prejudice. Is there any guarantee that this will work?

Bimal said – it may be strange to you but I have to try anything which has any potential to relieve your mother's pain and suffering. I just cannot stop trying until your mother gets well, I want to see her healthy and well, I shall not stop until she is well and happy. He stopped speaking.

Both of his sons argued – daddy, this is all nonsense, it is difficult to see that our father believes in this type of old and prejudiced performance which has no scientific basis. We do not think it is going to help mom, however, we shall let you know our opinion about it in a few days if we want to participate in this kind of rituals.

Bimal explained to them that whether his children agree with it or not he was going to perform it anyway even if he had to do it. He was up for it and it would be done in a week or so and he wanted his children's decision by that time.

In the meantime Bimal's children had a discussion among themselves about this ritual. The elder son said to his brother and sister – I don't understand why daddy is after me for this atonement. This old time prejudice has consumed daddy, how I can make him understand that I do not want to do it because if I do it, according to daddy I shall be responsible for any sin committed by mother. I don't even know what she has done or not done and I have to be responsible for it. If mom is sick and suffering what I can do, that is not my fault. But who is going to speak to daddy about it.

Younger brother responded – tell daddy that you cannot do it. I am not going to fall for this nonsense. My answer to this is plain no. I don't care what daddy thinks, I simply cannot do it. I shall let him know my decision only if he asks again, I am not volunteering now, I shall simply keep quiet.

Their sister was very upset with the brothers' reluctance for doing this ritual. She said – you guys are very selfish, mom did so much for us since the day we were born and you guys do not help her in sickness. This is very selfish. I wish I was her son, then at least I could do it for my mother's health and comfort.

Please rethink your decision and give daddy a moral support and take his pain away. Brothers, you are opting for a real selfish act, please do not do it, help our parents. God will bless us. Let's be grateful to our parents.

Both brothers reacted to her – stop the lecture, since you do not have to do anything you are giving us lecture, stay out of it, we will do whatever is best for us. Mom is dying anyway, what is the point for all these? Let her die in peace. You think we don't feel for mom, you are wrong, we love her too, and she is our mother too, only we do not want to succumb to any superstition or dad's importunity. You are our little sister, stay that way, do not try to interrupt in our business, let us handle it our way, no more discussion about it, We will do what we think is the right thing at this point.

Parents bring the children in this world and leave no stone unturned to raise them well, give them good moral values yet some of the children turn out to be the most selfish and mean personalities, as a parent you are helpless, cannot do anything to avoid this situation, because already they are adults. You can only sit back and regret and think what you could do different so that they were raised to become a better human being. Bimal was in the same situation, his wife Aruna and Bimal tried their best, gave them enough love, affection, always tried to instill moral and human values in them, yet two sons turned out to be mean and selfish while the daughter grew up to become a loving and compassionate person. Bimal and Aruna both were very kind and giving, their children grew up in this environment yet they have no feeling for others, not even for their parents, this always bothered Aruna and Bimal but they could not do anything about it but to endure the frustration and pain for it. When these two sons got married Aruna and Bimal bought them separate houses for them and they were living separately since then. However, occasionally they would visit their parents and spend some time with them. The daughter got married to a person who was living in USA and she moved to USA to live with her husband. The daughter was different from the brothers, kind and helping like her parents. She would visit her parents every other year and spend sometimes with her parents in their house. Bimal and Aruna would spend those days very happily with their only daughter and her son, their only grandchild.

Bimal waited for their sons' response to his request for doing the ritual but time passed by, he did not receive any answer from them. His mind and heart became intense with touchy feelings, he could never imagine that his own flesh and blood could be so irresponsible and defying that they would not get back to their father about this commencement, he thought they should have at least let him know that they did not agree with their father's desire. With emotion and pique heart he remembered the old days when Aruna was well and she always said – do not expect anything from the children, when they grow up they will have their own world which may not have any place for us, if it happens, let it go. Do not be sad, just let that go and thus we will not have any ill feeling about the children.

A few days letter Bimal went to the Priest and said – I am arranging for the worshipping for my wife. Also I want to perform the last rituals for myself because I do not want that any of my children bear the responsibility of doing this last ritual for me, I want to make them free, they do not have to bear any responsibility for my last rituals, since I can do it myself, I do not want to involve them. This is my last wish.

Priest replied – please let me know the date, I shall be at your home with all the accessories for performing the last rituals and we shall do it in a decent manner.

Bimal came back to his house and called his lawyer. He has decided to make a will for his properties and possessions. He started to deliberate how he is going to distribute his wealth among the peoples who worked for him, he decided to donate his factories to the employees, every employee including his residential employees will receive equal percent of the ownership of the factories, his residence will be turned into an orphanage, all other assets were put into his charitable trust, he decided not to leave anything for his children except the houses where they live. However, he left some money for all the grandchildren because he thought they are very special to both Aruna and him, this much he could do for them anyway, after all Aruna and Bimal are none but their grandparents.

A few days later in a morning Bimal performed the rituals of his life for the wellbeing of Aruna and their after death would be ceremonies and he felt much better that finally Aruna's sufferings will come to an end. For him the whole procedure was not a superstition but a real boon for the ailing person, he believed in it, Aruna believed in it, and that's all mattered at that time. Beliefs may bring about miracles in anyone's life and exactly that happened in Aruna's life. She felt much better and told to Bimal – Bimal, time has come for me to depart this mundane world, although I am feeling lot better but I know it is not going to last long, I can foresee the end of the tunnel where a beautiful divine world is waiting for me. Bimal, thank you very much for sharing such a good life with me, I am grateful for having me as your wife and spending the life together, I shall wait for you on the other side of life, with the hope to join you when you come there. Bimal said – Aruna, please stop. You have made my life a glittery star, only with your help I could become whatever I am today. I am thankful to god and grateful to you for supporting me when I needed one, for helping me when I needed the most and I always felt that journey of my life will be a consummate example of love and respect for our conjugal life. No more talking, take rest and go to sleep. I shall be sitting here and watch you go to sleep. Nobody knew that Aruna went to sleep for eternity, with God's blessing she passed away in her sleep, Bimal's faith and belief came to be true, his wife went to the place where she will mingle with the almighty and her soul will receive the peace and salvation. Now Bimal is relieved, he has nothing to look for behind, nobody to look after. He is a sad free man, loneliness became deep, yet he was strong and decided to follow his decisions about his life now.

A few days gone by, his children never came back to him to let him know about their decision of atonement for their mother. Bimal realized it deep down his heart that his children would never agree with Bimal's beseeching for their mother. Bimal called his attorney and instructed him to write the will, donating his properties and possessions to all of his employees and charitable organizations of his choice. Although his mind was restless and stormy but his heart was calm and cold as iceberg. He is happy that he does not have to be here anymore, he can fly anywhere like a bird in the blue sky. He sat down and took a paper and pen, he has to write a letter to his children for the last time, no more family or children, only him and his newly found freedom.

He started to write –

Dear children,

You have shown enough of your love and caring for your mother by not responding to my request for performing the "Prayoschitto" (atonement). You have disrespected a mother whose love and sacrifice gave your life, she always put you guys ahead of her life, when you were hungry she fed you, when you were sick, she spent many sleepless nights to comfort you, when you were scared, she gave you assurance and courage to overcome, she dedicated her life to raise you all once you were born. Your happiness was always her priority, your upbringing to a decent human being was her dream, and she did everything in her power but did she succeed? Could she inculcate the seed of decent human beings in her children? Only your heart and conscience have the answer.

According to our will, our properties have been distributed equally among our employees, as an employee of the company you will also get equal share of the distribution. We have left some money for our grandchildren, if you accept it, then give it to them when they become adult. Remember I did not inherit anything, I earned it and I did it very honestly. In your case, you have received your residence and company shares from your parents, now it is up to you how you are going to earn financial success.

We have failed miserably with you all. Now I shall set out to help young people to become a man with human qualities and human values. This way I shall perform my atonement for the failure we incurred in raising you all. Do not waste your time to find me out because I am not interested in you anymore. If you ever hear the news of my death, do not try to do the final rituals because I have already done it for your mother and myself and that was the most important final ritual of my life. Pain and agony made my life burdensome, now I shall start the journey of my life to undo the wrong doings. My best wishes for you all.

Next morning, he called all his household helps and said – from tomorrow you do not have to work for me in this house because I am not going to live in this house anymore. All of you will be employed in our factory from now on. Here is the deed for the land which I have bought for four of you, you can build your house in this land. Then he handed over four packets to each of them and said – this packet has the money for building your house, use it wisely and you will have a decent home for yourself. I thank you very much for the services you have rendered for my family. I pray for your wellbeing to lord Shiva "Stay well".

After Bimal's words one of the help told – sir, although I am a servant but you always treated me with respect, love and affection, your wife always took good care of me, being unmarried, I always reckoned your wife and you as my only family, I do not want land or money, please don't take away the privilege to serve you, I want to spend rest of my life taking care of you, please don't disappoint me. He prayed to Bimal with his hands folded. His eyes became watery, he started to break down in tears. Perfect example of love, affection, respect and mutual understanding.

Bimal listened to him carefully and said – my family and I are grateful to you for the service and dedication you have bestowed on us, I don't know where I shall go or what I shall do, I cannot put you in such uncertainty, I promise, if I ever need any help you will be the only person I shall ask for. For now, please do not insist on it. If we have ever hurt your feelings during your service here, please forgive us, we beg your forgiveness, he folded his hands and bowed to them to convey his respect. One other request to you all – please pray for the salvation of Aruna's soul. Then he embraced each of them one by one and bid them good bye. So many years' of love and togetherness are coming to an end. In the wake of sunrise of tomorrow Bimal will leave his house which was like a temple to him, this temple has lost its goddess none but his beloved wife Aruna. Now Bimal will enter into a life where the whole world will be his family, as a member of that family he will dedicate his life to create not only men but decent human beings too. Now he is going to prepare for the destination of tomorrow.

WALKING ALONE

——

W e all know that Americans suffer from various maladies
like Diabetes, high blood pressure, high cholesterol
etc. Statistically Cancer and Brain tumors also have taken a
detrimental position in our Society. In this shuffle of Statistics
one disease is always forgotten, that is the disease of mental health.
One can be physically very healthy yet mentally handicapped
in so many ways, consequently suffering all his or her life from
the agony of this disease. It is a hard reality that Government
ignores, medical community could give more importance to
it but for some reason they are also somewhat silent about it,
although a few Psychiatrists are trying to treat these diseases but
it is too little and too late. In the early eighties Federal and State
Governments tried to put a grip on this mental issue and had
opened a few Group Homes where these unfortunate victims
were placed and they were being trained how to maintain their
personal Hygiene and mingle with the general population.
Unfortunately, Budget Cuts have taken its toll and the care
for these mentally ill peoples were diminishing steadily for
the last decade. The mental disorder can be categorized in

different types, namely Clinical Depression, Anxiety Disorder, Bipolar Disorder, Attention Deficit/Hyperactivity Disorder, Dementia, Schizophrenia etc. Our communities should come forward to address this issue so that our young people do not suffer anymore.

It is also seen as a Stigma and the most of the family members do not want to admit its existence in their families and sometimes they do not even understand the gravity of the disease or its consequences. Now a days it is spreading alarmingly under the current of normal ailing regimen and lots of our young peoples are falling prey to these mental health conditions. It is also penetrating in Indian Communities where I have seen so many young children of our community are becoming victims of this deadly conditions. I have experienced death of known children and adults who were suffering from these conditions. One such victim was in the patient list of my Drug Store. Her name was Deborah Miller, commonly known as Debbie. She was a seventeen year old and a very beautiful white girl. Her well behaved manner was praiseworthy and I have enjoyed to converse with her all the times. Her mother and grandmother were also regular customers in my Pharmacy. Normally Debbie's mother used to come to fill Debbie's prescriptions and she always expressed her concern about her daughter. She used to say "Debbie is an excellent student, she sings well, every teacher loves this soft spoken polite young lady, unfortunately her mind does not work properly, and as a result sometimes she does things which cannot be expected from a girl like her. Honestly my mother and I try so hard to keep her mind in order but we cannot keep up with her and suddenly she behaves very erratic and becomes unpredictable. "

I used to quell her mother by saying "please make sure that she takes her medicine regularly and does not skip any dosage, it is very important and make sure that she does not miss any dosage at all."

Her mother said "that is the biggest problem I face every day. She does not want to take medicine at all. She always complains - why she has to take this every day? Why she cannot become like other girls, what did she do wrong? Also the effect of these medicines does not make her fill good and she feels dozy." It became very clear to me that she wanted to become like any other girls of her age, she did not want to accept that her mental composure is different than others. This is a very legitimate question for any young lady who is gifted with everything other than a good mental health. I realized probably her Psychiatrist could not explain the condition to her properly and after the treatment she will be cured and she will become a regular teenager again. I told her mother "please bring her to me when you come to fill her prescription next time. I shall speak to her about this issue. Hopefully she would understand her prognosis.

In this country, almost all the businesses are slow except tourist industry and some fast food restaurants. My business was slow, I had enough time to have a cup of coffee. So, I asked my help to fetch me a cup of coffee. When she came back with the coffee she was breathing heavy and told me - "one girl is walking naked in the street; everyone is looking at her. All men have surrounded her and watching her with lust. Some of them are leaking her with their eyes, it is disgusting. The woman is completely naked from head to toe."

"Do you know the girl?" I asked her.

"Yes, I know the girl. She is our customer. I don't know her name." She replied. I stopped drinking my coffee and ran out of the store to witness who that girl was. I knew, she must be someone who was using antipsychotic or antidepressant drugs. She might be hallucinating and might have no idea what she was doing. When I was walking to that direction, I found a tall white young lady walking slowly with a vacant look in her eyes and murmuring words very slowly and curious crowd was looking at her with lustful interest. Their lustful eyes were sipping every drop of her naked beauty. She was surrounded by a few persons, some were watching from behind, I went close to her and found out she was my patient Ms. Deborah Miller. She had no idea what she was doing or saying. I looked at the crowd and said – "please move away, how come you are not helping a sick woman instead surrounded her as if you guys are watching a circus. I rebuked." I took off my Pharmacy Jacket and covered her body and asked – "Debbie, please come with me. What happened, you came out of the home without wearing any cloth. Please come to the pharmacy, I shall call your mom, she will take you home." She did not react to my words. She was under the influence of some heavy drug or drugs. However, she followed me to the pharmacy. I asked one of my assistants to keep an eye on her and call her mother, Ms. Ana.

"Ms. Ana, I am calling from the pharmacy, your daughter

Debbie is in the pharmacy, please bring her clothes and the rest I shall let you know when you come to the pharmacy." I told her.

Ms. Ana came to the pharmacy a few minute later and saw her daughter sitting in my office wearing my long dispensing coat. Perplexed by the situation she held me and started to cry. "I did not know that she left the house naked. I was in the bed room cleaning and when I finished, I did not see her; I thought she went out for something. I could never think that she left the house naked." She stopped.

"Doc, I thank you very much for saving my daughter; for saving the honor of my family from the bottom of my heart. God bless you and your family." I found water in her eyes. She was very sad.

"It's over now. Take her home. I am sending Sandy with you to make sure that you go home without any trouble. Make sure she takes enough rest when she goes home. In a few days she will be alright."- I told her. Debbie and her mother left the pharmacy for their home. I had a sigh of relief that I could save this girl from harm's way.

Few days later Debbie came to me and said – "I thank you very much what you have done for me the other day. You have saved me from a bunch of lusty wolves. You have done the job of my father. I shall never forget you for saving me and my family's dignity. I am very grateful to you." She expressed her gratitude to me.

"Debbie, you are ill with a disease of your brain. Your brain is not producing certain chemicals in proper ratio. These chemicals are needed for proper brain and mental function.

That is the reason Doctor has prescribed medicine, if you take them in proper way, very soon you will be cured and start functioning normal. I also want to remind you that it is not your fault that you have this disorder, sometimes it just happens to certain individuals. Just try to ignore it. You are very pretty and smart, try to make good use of the gift, god has given you, make your family proud of you." I advised her. She gave me a beautiful smile which indicated that she accepted my explanation.

Then she said "sometimes I feel very bad and at that time I do things which are out of my control and also do all kind of wrong things. I wish, it did not happen to me. Honestly I do not know how to abstain from doing these bad things."

"Normally, in life if one door is closed, the almighty also opens another door for escaping. Life is a very valuable gift of God, please try to preserve and protect it. Do you know any specific symptom which triggers these episodes?"

"I do not feel the exact symptom every time but they are very similar in nature and I can understand that something is going to happen to me" – Debbie told me in a despaired voice. "I wish I knew when exactly it is taking place" – she added. I could feel the desperation in her voice. I felt that she was crying out for help so that she does not have to go through the same ordeal again.

"I shall try to remember your advice. I thank you again." She confirmed her gratitude.

One thing in this country, time never hangs heavy on anyone. It comes fast and goes fast. Today's events become history tomorrow, then people forget completely about it. Eventually this event became nonexistent in my mind, I forgot about it. My regular life took over my daily business. Surprisingly, a few years later, Debbie came to my pharmacy one day and wanted to see me. I was very glad to see her; she was well groomed and well dressed. She came to me and said – "do you remember me? I am Debbie, whom you saved one day from those lusty wolves. Anything could happen to me that day if you were not there for me. I am very grateful for the advice you gave me about my disease and now I realize how meaningful and helpful that was to me." She smiled and she looked very happy.

"What are you doing now" – I asked her.

"I have finished my Master degree in Sociology and I have joined a hospital in their social services department. I work with different patients for their different needs which arise out of their disease and social needs." – She replied. Smilingly she added – "you will be glad to hear that now I have formed a Support Group with my friends for the mentally disabled peoples. I want to make sure that nobody suffers or goes through the things which I went through. One day you opened my eyes and I thought it would be pretty cool to follow your advice and act accordingly. Whenever I feel bad, I try to remember your advice and try to overcome the obstacles and regroup myself for my daily life; and it always works. Thank you very much for giving your helping hand to me and my family."

"Debbie, I am very glad to see that you are pursuing your dreams, someday you will succeed. God bless you." I was overwhelmed by her transformation to a higher level of her life. "God gave you the life, if you can change one life to a better, your birth as human being will be consummate with happiness and joyfulness" – I spoke to her.

Debbie listened to me very attentively and said – "I shall always remember your advice." She then took out a beautifully wrapped box from her bag and said – "I have brought this for you. Please accept this and use it every day when you are in the pharmacy. I did not return the apron with which you covered my body that day, that apron is a souvenir and inspiration to me, with your permission I want to keep it." She became very emotional and I could see her eyes were watery with emotions, love and gratefulness. I thought her gift was my life's greatest present and valuable recognition of my professional life. I accepted the package very happily and embraced her and said "thank you very much, it means a lot to me, especially when it is coming from you".

She looked very happy to hear my words and said – "I have to go now, my mom and grandma are waiting for me in the house."

"Debbie, please convey my good wishes and regards to your mom and grandmother" – I requested her.

She said – "I will do that. Thank you again for being there for me".

She gave me a hug and bade good bye to all of us in the pharmacy. I walked her to the door and envisioned a confident and brave young woman is walking away keeping her head high in the populous street of the neighborhood. I felt – we need more hero like her. I blessed and prayed for her happiness.

(Names used are not real)

BANGA SAMMELAN

—

When the USA opened the immigration to the Asian countries in sixties, a large number of Bengalis from India started to migrate to the United States of America. After couple of years, these immigrants felt that there is an emptiness in their lives for cultural and social activities. Then they started "Durga Pooja Festivals" and there would be musical and cultural functions during those Durga Pooja days. Then came "Sarasvati Pooja" and "Kali Pooja". The newly immigrated Bengalis started to feel that their lives in this newly adopted country were becoming richer and happier in every sphere of life. But these seasonal celebrations were for a few days on a very temporary basis. They started to think about for some more meetings and chats on a more frequent basis.

Normally, by nature the Bengalis are very cordial and friendly peoples. They love to socialize with friends and families and also enjoy good food with friends and love to raise a storm on the coffee cup about politics and politicians. These new immigrants were missing this socializing part of life and they thought that they should do something to fill this vacuum in their lives. After many discussions they came to a decision that they would create an association or club to fulfill their chatting and meeting appetite of their minds. Finally, they established an association and named it as "The Cultural Association of Bengal" and it was registered with the Education Department of New York State on Nov 21, 1974. They were very happy to create this Association and were happier to have a potential to whet their cultural and social appetites. Then their creative minds came up with an idea of doing a "Bengali Conference" named "Banga Sammelan" in USA where they would bring the musical performers, dancers, writers etc. from Kolkata. The first "Banga Sammelan" was held in the 4th of July weekend of 1981 in New Your City and close to two hundred peoples attended the first "Banga Sammelan". The seed of this Conference started to grow bigger and bigger every year with the attendance of more and more participants. This growth was steady and spectacular, this little plant eventually became a big historic tree. Now a days this is the biggest and most enjoyable festival of the Bengali Community in the USA. In the beginning CAB used to run this North American Bengali Conference (in short NABC) every year, as it started to grow bigger and bigger it started to become difficult for CAB alone to run this year after year. After many deliberations CAB management decided to spread this NABC in different cities of USA and also decided to offer other Bengali Associations of different cities if they would be interested to hold this NABC in their respective cities. So, according this decision management of CAB started to call many Associations and most of those Bengali Associations agreed with this proposal, and why not, because to hold a Banga Sammelan is very prestigious matter for any local Bengali Association, and since then Banga Sammelan has spread all over the USA and Canada. Eventually Banga Sammelan went to west to cities like Los Angeles, San Francisco, Las Vegas, in south cities like Houston and Orlando, in north, cities like Chicago, Boston and in Toronto of Canada, NABC became very famous in USA and West Bengal of India. The aroma of fame of Banga Sammelan made CAB a very famous and coveted Organization in USA and West Bengal of India as ell. The cultural water of the river Ganges and Hudson started to flow together to reach the bay of cultural world of East and West and finally reach the ocean named Cultural Association of Bengal. The Banga Sammelan became the strongest pedestal of music, art, dance, drama, literature and performing arts of both West Bengal and Bangladesh in USA. Every year this union of culture of East and West is very adroitly done in the Banga Sammelan of the Cultural Association of Bengal, only Cultural Association of Bengal can accomplish such mega events of Banga Sammelan. Although now a days Banga Sammelan is hosted by different association of different cities, the Cab always helps the host Organization in every aspect of this mega event with CAB's expert experience, as a result at the end it rather becomes a joint operation together with CAB and the host Organization.

Similarly, the Banga Sammelan of the year 2018 was held by host Organization Ananda Mandir and CAB was the key organization to render help to the host Organization. As the President of the Cultural Association, I had the privilege of experiencing and working for this mega event very closely, one other feature of this event is that it is really a production of hundreds of volunteers who put thousands of hours of work and never get any remuneration for their work. CAB is doing this conference for last forty years, I do not know if any other ethnic group has ever organized any conference consecutively for so many years, maybe it is a record what CAB has done so far and so long. I must mention a few names of CAB predecessors who have dedicated their time and effort, Ranjit Datta, Prabir Roy, Kajal Sarkar, Purna Bhattacharya, Dilip Chakrabarti and most recent bearer of the torch are Milan Awon and Chitta Saha, CAB is grateful to these distinguished members whose vision has put CAB and Banga Sammelan to a new higher level and altar of excellence.

The 2018 Banga Sammelan was held in Atlantic City, sometimes known as one of the sin cities of North America. Once this city of glamour and fame never slept, but the recent economic down turn of gambling has made this a city of fiduciary disaster, neighborhoods turned gloomy and peoples are devoid of employment, happiness disappeared from the face of Atlantic City. But 29th June brought a Tsunami of roaring happiness in the mind of Atlantic City and the glowing brightness in the heart and face of this city by the presence of thousands of Bengalees who brought life in the hotels of Atlantic City. This was due to the presence of none but the North American Bengali Conference also known as Banga Sammelan. The Banga Sammelan of 2018 was held in the Sheraton Convention Center of Atlantic City. The decoration of the convention center was uniquely done by the host of this Banga Sammelan. This year's Banga Sammelan was hosted by Ananda Mandir of New Jersey along with Kallol and a few other Bengali Associations. This is the first time that a religious organization took the lead to host the Banga Sammelan of North America. From this point of view both CAB and Ananda Mandir took a historic decision to execute this Banga Sammelan of year 2018.

It will be pertinent to describe the decoration of the convention center. On the first floor of the Convention Center there was a beautiful combination of artistic beautification which is normally known as "Alpana" in West Bengal. Besides the beautiful decoration, entrance to the elevator was adorned like a gate where peoples would enter the elevator and go to different halls to enjoy the musical performances of all the artistes, in one side was beautifully decorated "Kulo" and on the other side was beautiful

In the evening of 29th June, 2018, the inauguration of Banga Sammelan was started with a very pleasing chorus sung by the members of Ananda Mandir. After the inauguration, all the spectators were welcomed by the national Anthems of USA, Canada, India and Bangladesh. These young singers performed to the perfect and highest level of musical tone. Among them Tania Roy Chowdhury was the best. She sang the national anthem of USA. She mesmerized everyone by her skill and sweetness of her vocal tune. May be a new star is born in this Banga Sammelan. After the national anthem Ashok Rakhit and Jay Prakash Sarkar of Ananda Mandir and Soumen Roy of local association named Kallol welcomed all the participants.

Final welcome address came from the CAB President Dilip Chakrabarti. In his short speech he reiterated the importance of "Banga Sammelan" in USA and emphasized that Banga Sammelan is like any big festival, religious or not in West Bengal, and this is imperative that Bengalees of USA must do it every year for whetting the cultural appetite and also to inculcate a deep affection and love of our cultural heritage to our new generation born and raised in USA. Anyway, these speeches only beckons that real deal is coming soon, and these also work as a catalyst in spectator's mind that the gala of celebration is imminent and going to take place soon. After this small initiation, the famous dancer, Sukalyan Bhattacharya of India began the bon voyage of Banga Sammelan. It was really astonishing to notice that this famous and highly skilled dancer put his show with a whole bunch of dancers whom he trained here in USA and produced his outstanding show which can easily be marked as one of the best shows he ever performed with his relatively unprofessional troupe.

Like every year, this year also arrangements were made for different seminars for Business, Medical, Literature etc. and the participants could partake in these free discussion. Medical seminar was conducted by Kallol Chattopadhyay, a famous Bengalee businessman. Dr. Kiran M. Das, Dr. Ashish Mukherjee, Prof. Debabrata Banerjee and Ms. Indrani Dhar. Moderator Kallol did an excellent job in running the Seminar.

Writers Srijata Bandopadhyay, Angshuman Kar, Shekhar Basu and Goutam Dutta of Kolkata were the stars in the Literary Seminar. In this seminar many Bengali writers of USA and Canada participated in reading their stories, poems etc. Once you hear their writing, it becomes evidently clear that these writers are very talented and someday their creation will glorify the Bengali Literature and Culture.

This year's Business Seminar has definitely made a special mark in the minds of participants by virtue of its excellence. Many dignitaries attended this meaningful seminar. Consul General of India, Sri Sandeep Chakravarty of New York and Governor Dr. Tathagata Roy of Tripura attended this seminar. But the whole show was stolen by Asha Rangappa of CNN and India's pride young talent Tanmoy Bakshi who is Honorary Cloud Advisor of IBM. Asha and Tanmoy won the heart and soul of the attendees by the depth, eloquence and felicity of diction of their speech. In recent year NABC never had such a successful business seminar as this one.

The main attraction of any Banga Sammelan is musical and cultural programs performed by the artistes of Bengal, India and North America. Also theatrical performance is an integral part of any Banga Sammelan and this year was not different either. This year's drama "Sat Phake Bandha" made the audience laugh to their hearts content, Sabysachi Chakrabarti and Chandan Sen were among the actors, and this drama definitely refreshed the mind of audience. Singers Shuvamita, Iman Chakrabarti, Shovan Ganguly and others have earned the praise of the peoples by their unique voice and musical performance. Anupam Roy's band also has fulfilled the expectation of the audience. "The Music Beyond Boundaries" has satisfied everyone's mental appetite. Last but not least the "Closing Ceremony" was deserves praise. Tabla Maestro Bikram Ghosh has orchestrated and performed in closing ceremony and no doubt his performance has raised this year's Banga Sammelan to a different higher level. Everybody was very satisfied to witness this talented maestro perform in this Banga Sammelan.

Although IBF's award ceremony became a reason for happiness some but to others it was kind of boring and monotonous. We congratulate to recipients of "Sera Bangali" awarded by Aaj Kaal, but the question remains "Sera Bangali" judged on what scale? Congratulations to the recipients of recognition award given by "Ananda Mandir" and "CAB". These recipients worked all their lives for the betterment of their community and culture in USA. Congratulations to the lucky person who has won the "P.C. Chandra Raffle".

The worst nightmare of organizer of Banga Sammelan is the Registration Desk. It is always filled with panic of failure as it is the first encounter with the registrants, if it goes well, Banga Sammelan goes well. Unlike every year, this year registration floated very smoothly, no crowd, no mistake, no anger, only smiling faces of registrants and volunteers who took care of the registration desk. Words "thank you and enjoy the programs" were flying in the air and happy faces were on the floor of this area. And the credit goes to IT expert Joy Bhowmik and Nilotpal Pal.

Two distinguished guests spent some time in CAB Booth. They are Governor Dr. Tathagata Roy and the Ambassador Mr. Sandeep Chakravarty. Dr. Roy is well known for his scholastic talent. He has written many books. Some of us were with them in CAB booth and engaged in Adda with them. Dr. Roy's wit, humor, wit and simple mind generate a deference to his personality. Ambassador Sandeep was so down to earth in his conversation, that I was wondering how this man could negotiate with so many renowned diplomats of the world. These two men along with CAB President Dilip Chakrabarti attracted a small crowd in front of the CAB Booth like flowers attract bees by its fragrance and beauty, so did they by their humble opinion, by mutual respect and vast knowledge of the current political situations of the world and their simple mind and smiling face they won the whole crowd close to the CAB Booth.

The volunteers are the pillars of any Banga Sammelan in any given year, this year also they were the soul and life of Sammelan. None of these conferences would ever be successful without their relentless hard work. This year was not different either, when everyone else is having fun, but these dedicated volunteers have no time for it, because they are busy in doing things so that the attendees can enjoy the whole stay with joyfulness and happiness. Simply such an example came to my notice, when everyone is talking, doing things of their own for fun, I saw, a lone lady by herself is helping everyone with a smiling face in a registration booth on both Saturday and Sunday mornings. Although sincerity, tenacity and dedication are rarely found in any human being now a days but this lady is a living example of these rare qualities as selflessness and sacrifice. We thank these volunteers and this lady in particular from the bottom our hearts for their sacrifice, without them there would be no Banga Sammelan.

In any Banga Sammelan, food becomes an issue of dissatisfaction, this year the reason for discontent was little different, complaint was food was good but quantity was not enough to whet the appetite. Also there was a complaint that most of the performances were late to start, timing was not maintained, sometimes, spectators lost their patience for this failure of timing. Later on it was found that one the reason for timing mess up was the sound system which failed to work perfectly; so more time needed to correct this problem, as result some of the functions started late, otherwise, in general besides a few short comings this Banga Sammelan was a very successful addition to its own history of NABC.

Nothing is lifelong, not even our Banga Sammelan, it has an end to it. Our beloved Banga Sammelan has an end also. The consummation of this year's Banga Sammelan was done by transferring the "Banga Sammelan Plaque" to "Sanskriti" a Bengali Association of greater Washington. We convey our congratulations and good wishes for their success in next year's Banga Sammelan.

In fine, it can be easily said that except a few short comings, this Banga Sammelan was joyful, successful and satiated and it also raised the bar of success to a newer and higher level of success. The credit goes to CAB and Ananda Mandir, the pilots of this voyage of Banga Sammelan, only their tenacity, hard work, sincerity, dedication and deep sacrifice could produce a Banga Sammelan of this magnitude which will be remembered many years by its spectators. Their yearning put the Banga Sammelan to a new altar of success. We, the spectators were spell bound by their imagination and execution of this Banga Sammelan. We sincerely thank them for producing an outstanding Banga Sammelan of this level of enjoyment like this.

At last, we, the spectators of Banga Sammelan, with our hearts content can roar at the top of our voice "Banga Sammelan, Jug Jug Jio" which means "Banga Sammelan Long Live".

ABOUT THE AUTHOR

Dilip Chakrabarti was born in the village of Jainpur in the district of Mymensingh in November of 1942 in undivided India, but his birth place is presently in Bangladesh territory. After freedom of India, when the riot broke out, his parents were compelled to leave their home to avoid atrocities of fanatics who tried to kill all the Hindus who were living in that region. As a result he moved to Kolkata with his parents. His family became extremely indigent and life became very uncertain for this uprooted family.

As a young child Dilip never enjoyed normal childhood. His family was struggling to make ends meet and he started to sell onion, garlic and few other small items in the local market in the early morning and evening. This was some help to his father's meager income. Poverty or starvation became part of their lives. But nothing could stop this young man from educating himself. His merit, hard work and determination drew the attention of teachers and they helped him with books etc. in his school days. After finishing his school, he finished diploma in Pharmacy, his B.A. and B.T. and eventually degree of B. Pharm from Jadavpur University, Kolkata, India.

He started his working life as a clerk in State Transport Corporation of Calcutta. He then moved to his pharmacy career working for the government of West Bengal. Being disgusted with corruption in government, being offered bribes many times he quit government employment and joined private sector as a pharmacist. In mid seventies he migrated to USA. In the beginning, life was full of struggle and hardship but he found his success eventually. He became a Civil Servant of New York State working for the department of Mental Hygiene. He always wanted to become self employed and eventually opened his own business where he found financial success and mental satisfaction of serving the ailing people. He soon realized that the happiness of his own life was not enough unless he can make a difference in other's lives. So, he started his philanthropic efforts to bring about changes in others' lives by his relentless effort of doing better to others. All his life he wanted to make a difference in his community. He felt a dire need of a place for a temple for the Bengalee community in New York City and vicinity. So, he became the instrument for establishing a Kali Temple even putting on the line his personal asset. He would not stop until the Kali Mandir in Baldwin is in good running condition.

He was inspired by his father's selfless efforts to do good to others when he was in Bangladesh. His father's advice to him was – always share your good luck with those who need it most. He followed his father's footsteps and established "Mrinmoyee Madhusudan Eye Hospital" in Nona Chandan Pukur in West Bengal, India. Some of his philanthropic activities are:

1. Scholarship Fund in Ram Krishna Mission in Kolkata
2. Scholarship Fund in Tappan Zee High School in Orangeburg, New York
3. Mrinmoyee Madhusudan Hall in Jadavpur University, Kolkata
4. Mrinmoyee Madhusudan Eye Hospital in Nona Chandan Pukur, 24 Parganas (N), West Bengal
5. Complete renovation of " Adya Nath Siksha Mandir" in Patipukur, a high school which he attended.
6. A Library Hall for Bharat Housing in Shyamnagar, 24 Parganas(N).

Besides the above his financial help goes to anywhere from Anath Ashram to Deaf Childrens' School.

He has received numerous awards and recognitions from different organizations for his philanthropic activities in New York and in India. Some of them are:

1. "UDAYAN" News paper of New York
2. "NEW YORK KALI MANDIR" of New York

3. "ADYANATH SIKSHA MANDIR" of Kolkata
4. "HUMAN SOCIETY FOR GROWTH" of Kolkata
5. "YUBA SHAKTI MISSION" of Kolkata
6. "RAM MOHAN MISSION PURASKAR for PHILANTHROPHY" IN 2005, (A GOLD MEDAL AND 5 LACS OF RUPEES)
7. "MICHAEL MADHUSUDAN AWARD" by Michael Madhusudan Academy in 2010.
8. EAST COAST DURGAPUJA ASSOCIATION INC. (ECDPA) RECOGNIZED FOR UNDAUNTED WORK FOR THE BETTERMENT OF THE COMMUNITY IN 2019.

He always had interest in literary works. As a student he was running a Wall Magazine in the sixties. Presently he regularly writes for the "UDAYAN" and "SANGBAD BICHITRA" two Bengali news papers of New York. His articles are also published by an English daily news paper called "ROCKLAND JOURNAL".

He has written two books, "MANUSH MAATIR" and "AMERICA, A DREAM OF DREAMS". His book "AMERICA A DREAM OF DREAMS" has been selected the best book by "MICHAEL MADHUSUDAN SAHITYA ACADEMY" of Kolkata.

Lightning Source UK Ltd.
Milton Keynes UK
UKHW040607211220
375245UK00025B/1101/J